An RSVP to Hernán Cortés: Doña Luisa de Estrada Tells Her Story

Kimberly A. Folse, Ph.D.

Dedication

This book is dedicated to my many Mexican students who have worked with me as their English language coach, some for more than five years. Through our conversations, I came to love their country and its history. I'm fascinated that the remnants of the Aztec culture still exist and that many people in Mexico today have Aztec ancestry. I can only imagine what it must have been like for the Spaniards who discovered this civilization in 1519.

Acknowledgment & Thank You

In particular, I would like to acknowledge and thank Ana Mari Buganza. She's an acclaimed art historian from Mexico specializing in sacred art. For the past twelve years, we have shared a love of art and the history of Mexico.

Author's Note

The conquest led by Hernan Cortés has been hotly debated for decades. From a conquest perspective, it was a tale of gargantuan proportions. From the conquered, those in Mexico, it is a different story. One culture, the Spanish, attempted to superimpose itself on the natives of the country of Náhuatl-speaking people: primarily Aztecs, but also Mixtecs, Otomi, and Mazahua.

It's difficult to find accounts of everyday life in the early 1500s, post-conquest. This story attempts to make real what life must have been like then from the perspective of the aristocratic daughter of the treasurer sent to New Spain by King Charles V.

In the 1500s (in Spain as in New Spain), marriage engagements among aristocrats were often made by parents when their daughters were twelve or thirteen. These were engagements to ensure social status and make political alliances. Marriages followed when the girls were around fourteen. Consummation generally didn't happen until the girl had her first period. Aztec girls were also married around the ages of thirteen or fourteen.

The search for gold was a driver of the conquest. When the

Spanish arrived in Hispaniola (Haiti/Dominican Republic), gold was there for the taking. The island's unique geology – it sits on a fault – created a significant upwelling of gold and copper. Gold contributes to the lion's share of the island's economy today. The conquistadors needed slaves, primarily for mining, hence the dark history of enslaving thousands of the indigenous of Mexico to replace the dwindling supply of local Indians. It was never-ending, as hard work and disease killed most within a year.

Because of Spain's luck in finding gold in the West Indies, they expected to find gold in present-day Mexico. When I calculated how much gold Cortés originally sent to Spain from Mexico, it was equivalent to the weight of thirteen of my Toyota mini-vans. Ironically, this huge quantity of gold never made it to Spain. In 1522, Cortes sent three ships, two loaded with gold (and other treasures of cloth, feathers, and jewels) earmarked to various dignitaries. The third ship contained personal items and his famous *Letters to the King*. The ships full of gold were pirated on their way to Spain, and the loot was taken to France, only to disappear. Today, substantial gold mines exist in Mexico, especially in the north.

Most know that diseases brought by the Spaniards decimated the Aztec population. Initially, waves of smallpox and influenza killed tens of thousands. Ten years after this story ends, beginning in 1545 in Mexico and part of Guatemala, the population was hit by what the Aztecs called *cocoliztli* (meaning pestilence in Nahuatl). The afflicted came down with high fevers, headaches, and bleeding from the eyes, mouth, and nose, with death in three or four days. Within five years, as many as 15 million people –eighty percent of the population-- was wiped out. It was only in 2018 that scientists used DNA to identify the culprit as *salmonella enterica* bacterium of the typhoid family. It's a consequence of contaminated food or water due to a lack of sanitation.

There are only six known codices from pre-conquest times that survive today. They are held in libraries in France, the United Kingdom, and Vatican City, Italy. None are in Mexico (that I can verify).

Perhaps you've found the title of this story curious. The Acronym, RSVP is French and didn't come into being until 1865. It translates to Respond if you please (Please Reply) and is commonly used to determine who has responded to an invitation. Its use here is to signify that Cortés invited many guests to dine with him, and some, those he had a vendetta with, ended up dead afterward. He was suspected of foul play for several deaths but was neither charged nor ever found guilty. There are some contested references to the fact that he was eventually charged with his first wife's death in a civil case.

Contents

Chapter 1

A First Love

My name is Doña Luis de Estrada. I was born in 1513 to a wealthy family in Cuidad Real (Royal City), Spain, an essential city for trade. In Europe, this was the Age of Exploration and Discovery. In my lifetime, Christopher Columbus discovered new lands across the Atlantic, and I was to learn and experience firsthand the New World of the Aztec Empire that Hernan Cortés had just conquered. My story starts in 1522 when I was nine years old.

In Spain, I lived a comfortable life surrounded by servants and tutors. We weren't royalty but close enough to be the beneficiary of its affiliations. My title, Doña, signified my social status. Though not part of the nobility, my parents claimed a connection to the former King and Queen of Spain. My mother's family was somehow connected to Queen Isabella, possibly through her daughter Joanna, with whom my mother corresponded, and my father, some said, was an illegitimate son of Kind Ferdinand. True or not, having a connection to the Crown endowed one with privileges and protections not available to most. The reigning emperor since 1516 was King Charles V.

My mother's full name is Doña Marina Flores Gutiérrez de la Caballería. She's from a family of merchants who traded mostly in wool and textiles. Her birth city is Almagro, an enclave of merchants known for their Jewish roots. The city is located within a day of Cuidad Real. Like many others with Jewish heritage, her family converted to Christianity and became known as *Conversos*. In 1492, all Jews were banned from Spain. As the Inquisition in Spain intensified, even *Conversos* were targeted and sentenced. Mother's family was given a special document from the Crown (Queen Isabella and King Ferdinand) that they had converted to Christianity over a hundred years ago and were, therefore, free of Jewish blood. This letter provided some protection from the Inquisition. However, her family faced accusations that their conversion was more recent, creating a tenuous, potentially precarious circumstance for my mother and her family.

My mother was a kind, intelligent, attractive woman with gorgeous hazel eyes. She married my father when she was nineteen. As an educated woman, she managed our household and all the family's business affairs and properties. In 1522, she was thirty-four, the mother of four surviving children. I was her secondborn.

My father, Alonso de Estrada, had always been connected to the Crown in one bureaucratic form or another, either as an administrator or leader of men in battle. He's from Cuidad Real. He was gruff and businesslike and not particularly fond of children. As a tall man and somewhat awkwardly built, he had big hands and feet, and a prominent jaw covered with a beard. When he married my mother, he was thirty-five. In 1522, he was forty-five.

****

Luis Alfonso, my brother, who was thirteen in 1522, and I spent much of our days with our tutors. Our favorite was Luis Cordoba, a young man, twenty-four years old. He was tall and slender with delicate hands. His long and full eyelashes were one of his defining characteristics. He sported a thin mustache and beard. We called him Señor to signify his status as our tutor. Brilliant for his age, we were taught the classics—Greek and Latin—as well as history and geography.

On a dark afternoon in September, Señor Cordoba arrived just after the servants had refreshed the fire that kept us warm and the candles that gave us light. We watched the fire's sparks flutter when Señor Cordoba flung the door open with such force that it hit the credenza and swung back at him, almost knocking him over. His curly hair was wet with rain. As he entered, he tore off his drenched cape and tossed it on a chair. We jumped to attention.

I remember how he checked to see that all the servants had left before speaking. As he walked toward us, he leaned in and announced that he would be leaving as our tutor. We were dumbfounded. I'm sure my brother was sad because he and Luis had become friends. Me? I was heartbroken; Señor Cordoba was the object of my first crush. I found him charming, witty, and very smart. He always taught us something fascinating. He'd pick up little gifts for me, trinkets, from street vendors. I saved each in a little carved wooden box hidden under my bed. I fantasized that one day I would marry him. Our history lessons included the love story of Queen Isabella and King Ferdinand. If she could love and marry, so could I someday. In those times, marriages of our social ranking were arranged by parents, usually mothers, when a girl was twelve to fourteen. Love was not a consideration. Señor Cordoba would certainly not be considered a suitable marriage partner.

He began to tell us the reason for his sudden departure with such agitation that he spoke in staccato phrases rather than complete sentences. At times, he clutched his vest, trying to contain his excitement. He said he would be off to the New World, just discovered by conquistador Hernan Cortés. It was a world filled with strange, exotic peoples, temples, and gold. That was the first time I heard of the famous man Cortés.

When? was our concern. He told us he would leave after our session to prepare for his voyage to sail in October. His concern was the fare. Thinking out loud, he said he felt he could work on the ship to pay for some of his passage. My brother said he had some coins he could offer, so he turned and rushed off to fetch them. Señor Cordoba and I were left alone. I rushed to him, sobbing, grabbing him by the waist. Upwelled words that surprised me. I asked him if I could go too. He was confused at first, not knowing how to answer.

My brother arrived and saved him from the awkward moment. Señor Cordoba hugged me as he might hug his sister, saying he would write as often as possible. There was no mention of taking me; I was crushed. My brother offered him a little leather pouch filled with coins, which he accepted, promising to repay him someday.

My brother wanted to know where this New World was. Señor Cordoba reminded us of his lessons on the exploits of Christopher Columbus, who thought he had discovered the Indies after sailing west for three months. Instead, it was determined that he had found a big island, an island now called Cuba. He explained that Cortés sailed from Cuba further west to discover an even bigger New World.

He said there was a rush of Europeans sailing there to hopefully get rich. And there was gold to be found! Next, my brother asked him what he would do there without money.

Señor Cordoba hesitated for a moment. Maybe the reality of his economic situation would be enough to keep him in Spain as my tutor. I couldn't imagine that they would need tutors in this New World. He then stated confidently that he would be a Letter Writer! Indeed, his talents would be needed, especially for the illiterate. With that, he excused himself and waved goodbye, asking the servants to take him to my mother, who had contracted his services.

I had only one hope: Señor Cordoba would write to me from

this wonderful new world, and I would write back. Perhaps when I was twelve or thirteen, when he was rich, my parents could arrange our marriage. He would have to be, or marriage would be out of the question.

Chapter 2
Cortés' Second Letter to the King

When news of Hernan Cortés' discoveries and the conquest of Mexico (1519-1521) became known, there was an explosion of opportunity for the people of Europe. For the rich, it was a chance to become wealthier, and for the rest, it was an opportunity to escape the chains of the feudal class; one could become a conquistador, a civil servant, a miner, a pig farmer, and hopefully, eventually, a landowner, that is, so long as you were not Jewish.

I remember it was late December when Father called all of us together in our dining room in the middle of the day—Mother, me, my sister Marina, and my brother Luis. Father was rarely home, and this summons surprised all of us, especially Mother. He told us he had an announcement to make. The King had appointed him Treasurer in New Spain, as it was then called, and we would sail there in three months. If we had things of importance to us, we should gather them together. We would not be returning to Spain.

Of course, my brother and I knew what he was referring to when he told us we were going to the New World, but we did not reveal what we knew. I was elated with the news. Once there, I could find Señor Luis Cordoba! I assume Mother knew, too, but she said nothing in response to his declaration.

The King had named Cortés as the governor of New Spain. In these early years after the conquest, the Crown was coming to terms with its need to provide oversight of Cortés, whose wealth, popularity, and power seemed to grow exponentially. The Spanish government needed someone they could trust to monitor and account for all the monies going to the colony, funds for the salaries of civil servants, the Christian frays, and their churches. Going to Spain, was discovered gold, the Crown's share, the royal fifth.

While many sought to venture to The New World, the Crown "ordered" my father to go. He was to replace Diego de Soto, who served as Treasurer until my father arrived. Father was given the option of leaving in either the Spring or Fall of 1523, the favorable westward sailing windows. He chose Spring, giving him enough time to sort out all his family and business dealings. His life, my life, was to change forever.

I recall the whirlwind of activity in our household. I watched servants pack our belongings in chests, remove our furniture, and roll up carpets. Mother and Father were constantly arguing, something unfamiliar to us. We covered our ears or made ourselves scarce to avoid overhearing them.

My little sister, Ana, who was just four, was sent to a convent. I was devastated when I found out that my brother Luis Alfonso was to be sent to live with relatives. My youngest brother,

Juan Alfonso, was also given to the care of relatives at the age of five. I became afraid of what was going to happen to me. Maybe I wasn't going after all. My little sister, Marina, then seven, and I found solace in each other huddled together on a bench seat in an alcove with a window overlooking our orchard, its trees bare, bracing against the dense bitter cold that had settled in.

Mother had been searching for us. I didn't want to be found; perhaps I was next to be sent off to another convent or relative. When she discovered us, she sat with us, each of us under an arm, and assured us we would be coming across the ocean with her and Father to the New World. My anxiety was replaced with the hope of reuniting with Señor Cordoba.

One evening in late January, Father arrived home, expecting to be served something to eat before retiring. We were finishing our meal, and the servants cleared our plates and set up a plate for Father. Marina and I were about to leave when I saw Father place a large, thin book on the table. With his hand, fingers spread atop the book, he commanded us to sit. I glanced at Mother, who nodded that I should comply.

Father pushed his plate away and drew the candelabra closer for better light. His chair grated against the floor as he pulled next to the table. He slowly opened a deep, red-bound book that he said was a gift from the King to acquaint him with his destination in New

Spain. The book was Hernan Cortés' *Second Letter to the King* detailing the conquest. With that, my ears perked up. Before me was a book written by Cortés, the enigmatic man Luis Cordoba had introduced me to.

He selected the page, opened it, and carefully creased it at the binding so it would lie flat. He pointed to the page with his index finger and said, "That is where we are going: Tenochtitlán (Ten o chit LAN), the Aztec capital."

I couldn't comprehend what I saw before me. There was a large blue circle with a green rim. Several strips connected the rim to the center. As I peered closer, it looked like boats in the blue area. I realized I was looking at a lake with a big island in the middle. The strips must have been connectors for foot traffic.

Father relayed how Cortes described the city when he first encountered it. I can't remember everything because it was such an unimaginable scenario. He said the city was vast and magnificent. In the middle was a square larger than the largest square in Spain, Salamanca. He said the city had many public squares and markets where more than sixty thousand people would come to buy and sell. I couldn't imagine such a large number. For sale were rabbits, deer, and little dogs they raised to eat, some cooked over wood or coal braziers. There were jewels, gold, silver, and brightly colored feathers. On some streets, there were apothecary shops with medicines and herbs. The Aztecs made many different-sized earthenware pots of excellent quality that were glazed and painted.

According to the *Letter*, there many religious temples filled with Aztec idols. The main ones had priests who never cut or combed their hair. The priests could not interact with women, nor were women allowed to enter the temples.

Mother was wide-eyed and grasped my hand, which only intensified my awe. With that, my sister and I were sent to bed. My mind was curious and eager to learn more about this New World across the sea. I tried to imagine what Luis Cordoba was doing. I longed for a letter from him so I could write and tell him I, too, was also going to the New World so we could meet again.

Chapter 3

To the New World

I had never seen the ocean before. As we got closer to the port of Seville, the principal seaport for voyages to the New World, I caught the salty smell of the sea. I lifted my head to take in the new, moist scent. Many vessels –probably thirty –bobbed up and down as the tide lapped the docks, creating a dizzying effect. We watched and waited for three days as our ship, a caravel, was loaded with goods of basic furniture, housewares, and clothing chests. Then, the ten or so crew loaded the food, water, and other provisions, along with two pigs that squealed and snorted at being jostled in a crate.

As we stood on the dock that morning, a messenger arrived, delivering letters to Mother and Father. I watched as my father shuffled through the documents. He hesitated and examined one, turning it over several times. He looked over at me, calling my name: "Luisa." I knew instantly that it was a letter from Señor Cordoba. In my mind, I was already in the New World, reunited with my tutor. I placed the letter in my bag, waiting for a time when I could be alone to open it.

There were forty passengers. Besides my family, there were several relatives from my father's side whom he selected to help him in his new role as Treasurer. Four Franciscan frays (friars) boarded to evangelize the New World. They were sent by King Charles V to save the souls of the natives by converting them to Christianity. I found them curious in their dingy brown robes and barefoot. All of them were clean-shaven, something I liked. The other passengers included civil servants—an accountant and a lawyer, some with wives–and several businessmen: a barber, a cobbler, and three blacksmiths (big, strong, burly men). There were no other children besides my sister and me.

Once on board, we were led to our cramped quarters below deck. Bunks hugged the ship's sides, one atop another, three high. We used our top bunks to store some of our belongings and the food we brought. My sister and I shared a bunk, as did my mother and father. The air was stifling; it was dank and dim. At least it was clean, including the bedding. Because we were a family of four, our accommodation included a table with a bench affixed to the floor. Mother resigned herself to the situation. I was surprised that Father didn't complain, even when the ship's captain came to greet him.

When the ship was ready to set sail, we were all on deck to watch the raising and unfurling of the triangle sails. It was magical as the canvases caught the wind and tugged at our ship. I hadn't realized how mighty the wind could be. We watched as the land slowly disappeared and we were surrounded by ocean as far as the eye could see. I felt like I was starting a grand adventure into the unknown.

When all the passengers were on deck, watching the sun beginning to set, I went below for privacy. I pulled Señor Cordoba's letter from my bag. There was my name, Doña Luisa de Estrada, in elegant handwriting. With anxious anticipation of words of expected ardor, I broke the wax seal and unfolded the letter to reveal its contents. It was concise. The salutation was rather formal, without a hint of affection, and I was disheartened. He wrote that he was still in Santiago, Cuba, working as a letter writer, as planned. His skills were in high demand, he said. The letters he wrote for his customers were always about money, mostly the riches to be made with investment. He did not expect to leave Cuba for the new colony for at least six months.

I examined the letter again to ascertain the date it was written--March 15, 1523. If everything went according to plan, we would arrive in the New World about the same time he would, mid-August or early September.

The voyage was supposed to take about three months. That seemed an eternity when there was nothing to do and nowhere to go. We started in good weather, the winds gliding our craft across the sea. After a few weeks, we grew accustomed to the rhythms of life onboard—when meals were provided -- if you can call hard biscuits and salt pork a meal—and how to use the latrine, where we were allowed to venture on deck and the prohibited areas. We were encouraged by the captain to walk and get fresh air every day. He didn't want any sick passengers.

I liked the Captain. He was short and stocky, with a big belly that jiggled when he laughed, and he was always laughing, making for a lighthearted voyage. When asked about the New World, he claimed it was a marvel to behold and that we would be surprised at every turn.

Mother and Father were pleased to have the chance to get to know one of the Franciscan Frays, Pedro de Gante. He was most engaging, and he liked children. He enjoyed talking to me, asking me what I thought about Jesus Christ and what I knew about the sacraments. Of course, I told him I had memorized all the prayers in my *Primer* in Latin and Castilian. After I recited one, he raised his thick, dark eyebrows in astonishment. I felt so proud of myself. Mother respected the fray and his teachings. Curious about the world we were about to enter and the people that dwelled there, we were open to any knowledge he was willing to share.

Initially, he and Father had a lot in common. I overheard them discussing the possibility that they might be related. They had both been in the King's court, though not simultaneously. After a few weeks, Father preferred to go below deck and study his book, so Fray de Gante spent most of his time with my mother. I was always welcome to participate in those discussions. Mother and Fray de Gante discussed his plans for building many churches and creating a trade school for the natives. Someday, he hoped to build a hospital. Mother thought he was brilliant, and I felt so, too. That voyage was the beginning of their life-long friendship.

Fray de Gante was genuinely concerned for the indigenous people in the new land. The more he talked about them, the more I looked forward to seeing them. I couldn't imagine how they could be so different from me. Their rituals of human sacrifice, which I heard about from Cortés' letter, seemed terrifying. Fray de Gante explained it as ignorance of the Lord.

Me? I loved to be on deck, observing the sailors at work inspecting the sails, ropes, and riggings. Mother assented to my freedom but required that I be tethered to some heavy object with a rope around my waist.

One of the young sailors, Gilberto, a burly, shaggy-haired nineteen-year-old who sailed back and forth across the Atlantic, making two trips east and two trips west, back to Spain every year, became like an older brother to me. He taught me how to tie the five essential sailing knots -- cleat hitch, rolling hitch, half hitch, anchor hitch, and the bowline. He also taught me the words to some of the songs, the sea shanties, that the sailors sang in the slow afternoons. I was named the ship's mascot! They called me, "Pequeña Sirena!" (Little Mermaid). This camaraderie made me feel like part of a larger family, not just an anonymous passenger on a ship.

We sailed for two months without incident, but one morning in early July, we woke to a spectacular sunrise of deep reddish-orange and yellow clouds. According to Gilberto, there's a seafarer saying: "Red at night, sailors' delight. Red in the morning, sailors take warning." We were alerted to expect bad weather and that all passengers would be battened below deck. There was to be no mass that morning.

We climbed into our bunks, expecting the worst. For three days, the wind howled. It seemed we were lifted by a mountainous wave of water only to be dashed to the bottom of a valley of salty brine. We could hear other passengers moaning and groaning and praying to God for our safety. I wanted to experience the storm above deck, but Mother assured me I could be first out of the hatch when we were safe.

Once the storm passed, the captain took stock of the ship's condition and checked all the passengers' well-being. We cleaned up our belongings, ejected from the top bunk, and strewn around the floor. The worst part was the stench of the pigs that permeated the entire ship. No one had been able to clean up their defecation during the storm.

Life aboard the ship soon returned to normal, except Mother confirmed she was pregnant, at least six months along. Father sat at our table, with a candle always lit, obsessed with his book. He spent hours reading about what to expect in this new world. He tried to get Mother interested, but she remained calm and focused on staying comfortable.

Chapter 4
Our New Home in a Native Village

For days, we knew we were getting closer to our destination by the number of birds following our ship. We were treated to numerous pods of porpoises gliding through the water alongside our ship like giant birds. The ocean in this part of the world had turned beautiful, light blue, and clear. We watched as sometimes the sailors would jump in, just for fun, waving at us up on deck. On that beautiful clear afternoon, the ship's captain announced, "Land Ho!"

By day's end, we landed in the port of Santiago, Cuba. There were many ships in the harbor. We had to wait until a space opened up for us. Santiago was not our final destination. The captain needed to let off some passengers and take on some new ones. My father's relatives were forced to disembark. The reason they were given was that in Santiago, there was a place for them to live. When my family was settled, they would be sent for. We couldn't leave our caravel; we could only observe the hustle and bustle on the docks, day and night. It never ended.

I wondered how to get Señor Cordoba a message if I couldn't leave the ship. Perhaps he had already gone to New Spain. I had to console myself since I had written back that we were headed for Tenochtitlán. Surely, he was smart enough to know how to contact me through my father, assuming he got my letter.

Hawkers came alongside our ship to sell and trade fruits and hats. They were a scraggly bunch who often had a barefoot, dark-skinned native woman with them. It was my first introduction to the indigenous population.

The passage from Cuba to Cortés' conquered land took us several days. We landed on the eastern Gulf coast in Villa Rica de la Vera Cruz (known today as Vera Cruz, Mexico). Everyone, even Mother and Father, stood on deck as we sailed ever closer; we didn't know what to expect.

It was surprisingly hot and sunny in early September but also very humid. The passengers, in mass, began removing layers of clothes. We ladies divested ourselves of our underskirts. The men took off their heavy vests. Some even removed their stockings, bearing hairy legs. The blacksmiths bared their naked chests, their back, neck, and arm muscles bulging. I had never seen a man so bare, so virile. My father, in comparison, seemed old and weak.

We were transported ashore in small boats rowed by almost naked dark-skinned men clad only in loincloths. These were the first male Aztec natives I encountered. I could see that my mother was embarrassed. A group of seven men sent by Cortés to retrieve us greeted us on shore. Father was easily identified because he was the only one expected with children. Another group of men gathered the

Franciscan frays, leading them away. Fray de Gante waved goodbye as he and the three other Frays walked single file, as was their custom, following a man on horseback.

The men's captain assessed the situation. Looking at my mother, now seven months pregnant and exhausted, he decided we would be taken to a nearby village until the baby was born. We were escorted to Huitzilapan (whit zil a PAN). One of the soldiers told us that in the Nahuatl native tongue, it means "in the river of hummingbirds." True to its name, there were hummingbirds of every iridescent color flitting about.

Our destination, Tenochtitlán, was two hundred miles inland over rough and steep terrain. Two-hundred miles? It sounded far away. Indeed, it was. We were told it would take two months to get there. Another two months? I was ready to go. I wondered what Señor Cordoba would do if he went looking for us and were not there. I almost asked my mother to let me catch up to the Franciscan frays. Then I realized she probably needed me to help with the baby's birth. In retrospect, I'm glad I didn't ask and stayed. My experience in Huitzilapan would define my love for this world and its people.

As we walked into the village, the natives stared at us; they had never seen Spanish children before! We stared back to see people so different from ourselves. Like the rowers on the boat, the men hardly wore anything at all, exposing their well-built bodies. They wore their thick and black hair shoulder-length. Many had adornments in their ears or noses. Most of the little children wore nothing. The young girls and women wore a cotton skirt and a long top that reached below the waist. Some had pretty red woven designs. They wore their hair down, parted in the middle, looking unkempt. I noticed there were a lot of villagers with pockmarks on their bodies and faces. A few appeared to be blind. We were to learn that smallpox had decimated the native population, halving it at least, in an epidemic that swept the country two years ago.

Father was shocked that we would live in what he considered a hovel. His protests about our living conditions were directed at the soldiers. The men's captain assured him our house would be cleaned and provided with new bedding, double what was standard. He had no choice but to accept the situation. The soldiers ordered the villagers to hurry and make ready our beds—on the floor! This time, we were shocked to see where we were to sleep. Father announced that he would sleep with Cortés' men and we were left to ourselves. Before we settled down, food was delivered to our doorway. There was no door, per se, just a heavy cotton cloth draped over the doorway to keep out moisture and bugs. Laid out before us was a large basket of many kinds of fruits we had never seen before. A plate of roasted meat, beans, and flat pancakes made from corn. We filled our bellies and went to sleep, happy to stretch out and not worry about hitting our heads on a bunk above us.

When we awoke the next day, the air was filled with a sweet eucalyptus-like aroma. Its source came from the corner of the room, where a little clay stove emitted a wisp of smoke. I would later find out the smell came from copal, a resin the natives used to keep mosquitos away. There were a lot of mosquitos!

As I ventured out, I saw many vacant houses in decay. I realized that the smallpox epidemic must have killed many here in this village. The thatch roofs of the empty houses were caved in, and the white stucco covering the exterior crumbled to the ground, making a perimeter line around the abandoned structures. Our house was one of the bigger houses and faced the central clearing.

My sister and I adapted quickly to freedom. We played all day with the local children, which meant helping them first do their chores. All native children were required to fetch water or wood for the fires, cut back encroaching vines, or pick up trash. Young native girls, even younger than me, cared for those younger than them. So, when we played, we were a group of about twenty ranging in age from ten to two. I learned quickly how to carry a child on my hip as if it were attached to me.

I felt happy. It was a different kind of happiness than I felt in Spain. Here, my happiness felt like sunshine. I met a boy about my age. His name was Tonatiuh (Ton uh TI uh), which means sunshine in Nahuatl. Perhaps it wasn't a coincidence that my feeling of sunshine was like Tonatiuh's name. He taught me his language, and I taught him mine! My mother thoroughly approved, knowing it could be months or even a year before my formal education could be restarted. God brought us here for a reason, she proclaimed.

Father had nothing to do in the village except wait for the baby. He spent most of his time mingling with the soldiers. They had more in common; Father had been an admiral in the Spanish army.

While we waited for the birth, Cortés' men told stories of their brave and heroic leader, Hernan Cortés, and how he outmaneuvered Moctezuma, the Emperor of the Aztecs. They described Tenochtitlán's appearance when they first saw it three years ago. They made it sound like it was a great city in Heaven. Their words evoked the image I had seen in Father's book, and their descriptions made it sound more significant than it looked on the page. They said the city had many wide roads, more extensive than any in Spain. They estimated it was a city that was bigger than any European city.

The men described Aztec festival days, where many thousands would fill the streets and the grand plaza. On some of these festival days, there would be human sacrifices. That was something Father had not mentioned. They said Aztec priests would place a screaming sacrificial person on a large stone altar, recite an incantation and then proceed to slit open the victim's chest with a sharp obsidian knife and lift their heart out. Women, as well as men, were sacrificed. The image was horrific. I couldn't imagine these people engaging in such brutal acts against their people. Why would they do that, I wondered. It must be ignorance, as I remembered what Fray de Gante had told me.

What came next were tales of destruction and conquest. We listened as the men described the city's siege, the battles with the natives, and the ruler, Moctezuma. Many of the temples were toppled. The men assured us that sacrifices were no longer allowed. We were mesmerized.

I was enthralled by the story of Cortés' pet jaguar, which they said Cortés kept in his palace and allowed to roam freely. I knew about jaguars. They were in the jungle surrounding us. The villagers warned my parents that we must stay within the confines of the village lest a hungry jaguar stalk and take us away. The villagers worshipped the jaguar as a god, but it was also feared. According to the men, Moctezuma also had pet jaguars. Father thought having a wild animal like that free in one's home was ridiculous. I thought it was more than curious; it was remarkable.

To me, it seemed that Cortés touched everything. I wondered when I would meet this powerful man. Cortés' men frequently reverently mentioned their leader. Cortés. Cortés, Cortés, Cortés. Might Cortés be the king of this land? This was a thought that I intuitively knew my father would not appreciate.

Chapter 5

A New Baby in a New World

I remember the cool, quiet, fresh early mornings. Mother and my sister were still asleep one morning, but I was ready to start the day. Shimmering through the trees was a brilliant golden sunrise. Dew sparkled on the leaves from the moist night. In the distance, birds and monkeys screeched. Zipping around me were hummingbirds. Ducks and dogs roamed around the houses, looking for discarded edible tidbits.

I was still in my nightgown. I remember feeling the threshold's cool, carbon-rich packed earth underfoot. I had taken to going barefoot to Mother's mortification. But in her condition and given the situation, she relented. I inhaled, taking in what seemed like the whole world in one deep breath. I thought this world was wonderous!

The children of the village didn't get up that early. My friend, Tonatiuh, was still asleep. I stepped out and wandered into the common area. Xitlali (Zit LA li), Tonatiuh's mother, was working over a fire. She looked up and smiled. She was making corn tortillas, what I thought were pancakes. She showed me how to roll the ground corn into a ball and flatten it to make a tortilla. She placed them over the fire to give them a light toast, bringing out their deliciousness. They were especially good with beans. I loved them, as did my mother and my sister. Father was stubborn. All he wanted were hard-tack biscuits he'd beg from the soldiers. My family would wake up any minute, so I returned to our house before I could be missed.

It rained that afternoon. The village was calm as everyone retreated indoors. Laughter could be heard occasionally as the villagers chit-chatted to pass the time. I sat on the floor with Marina and Mother, playing a game similar to rock, scissors, and paper. My mind wandered here and there. I looked at my very pregnant mother. If we were in Spain, she would have had many attendants. I knew that giving birth was a dangerous endeavor; many women have died in the birth process. I told my mother that she needed a midwife. The subject had come up before, and Father was against it; he didn't want pagans, as he described the indigenous population, to have anything to do with the birth of his child. I didn't want to go against my father, but I needed a way to get him to change his mind. If anyone could convince him, it would be the captain overseeing Cortés' men.

I observed the captain from afar, huddled with his men under a makeshift shelter; Father was engaged with the men, unaware of his surroundings. I waited until the captain left the group and walked to one of the native homes. I quickly went to the house where he had entered and waited just outside. I was drenched; rain dripped steadily from the tip of my nose. It was cold, and I was shivering.

An RSVP to Hernán Cortés: Doña Luisa de Estrada Tells Her Story

When the captain emerged from the home, his head down to look where he was going, he almost crashed into me. Surprised, he barked, asking me what I was doing there. I pleaded my case and asked him to convince Father of the necessity of a midwife.

He was an astute man. In charge of the safety of my family, he quickly asserted that he would take care of the matter. Then, he sent me home. The next day, an Aztec midwife, known as a tlamatlquiticitl (tlah-maht-lkee-tee-SEETL), came to our house late afternoon. She paused briefly at the doorway, introduced herself, and walked in with authority. Under her arm was a large bundle of cloth and a bulky woven bag filled with all the implements of her trade. She surveyed the abode and then proceeded to examine my mother. Mother was skeptical, asking me how the visit from the midwife had come about.

I was about to explain when Father entered. Seeing what was underway, he asserted that I should fetch him once the baby was born. With that, he turned and left.

Xitlali, my friend Tonatiuh's mother, was summoned to assist. Led by the midwife, I watched while they cleaned the house and performed rituals and incantations to ensure a successful birth. On the third day, Mother went into labor. I didn't know if I should stay or go. Xitlali indicated I should stay. To my surprise, Mother thanked me for being there for her.

First, they bathed and washed her hair. This was the first time I had seen my mother completely naked. I saw her as frail compared to native women. The lightness of her skin, my skin, was so different from the earth color of these people. Xitlali gave my mother one of her typical native tops. It was clean and fresh. It's incredible how garb from another culture can differ yet provide the same function.

Even though this was my mother's seventh birth, her labor came on fiercely. She groaned as the frequency of her contractions increased. The midwife, prepared for any contingency, opened her bag filled with provisions, looking for the herbal drugs used for pain relief. Mother hesitated at first, but with Xitlali's encouragement, she consented. It worked!

I watched the birth with fascination. It was a girl! My little sister oozed out of my mother's womb into the hands of the midwife. I shouted with joy. "Mother, it's a girl!" The newborn was bathed and swaddled. Meanwhile, the midwife chanted to protect it from evil. She evoked the goddess Chalchiuhtlicue (Chal-chee-weet-lee-KWAY), the Aztec goddess of rivers, lakes, freshwater, and the baptism of children. She was known as the goddess "Who Wears a Jade Skirt." The purpose was to wash away the parents' sins from their newborn. I listened, only catching a few words. It would be many years later before Xitlali had enough Spanish to explain the ritual that occurred that day.

Xitlali handed me the baby. Looking down at the child, I felt a rush of maternal instincts. It would not be long before I would be of childbearing age. Mother looked on and exclaimed, "Mi Dulce," which means, "My Sweet."

Mother named her Beatriz. She was born in late November 1523 (I had lost track of days). When Father was informed about the birth, he arrived with the captain. It was a remarkable coincidence, said the captain. He told us that Cortés' native mistress had a baby boy almost a year ago --last January 1523! Father raised his eyebrows at this new information. I didn't know why Father reacted that way. I assumed it was yet another reference to Cortés. During our time in Huitzilapan, Father's disdain for the conquistador had grown.

According to the men, the native woman was famous in the New World; Cortés had used her as an interpreter and guide for the conquest. Her name was Marina. I was amazed to hear of a native woman with the same name as my mother and sister. I asked how that could be. The captain chuckled and explained that her name was originally Malintzin, but Cortés renamed her at her Christian baptism. He said Beatrice was probably the first full Spaniard born in the colony because there weren't many European women. I asked if Cortés' son was the first mixed-race child. He doubted that. With so few Spanish women in the colony, many European immigrants had taken up with native women. There were probably many children born of these unions. Some years later, they were to be designated as mestizos.

I wanted to know more about this son of Cortés and the native woman, such as his name, where he was born, and if he would be in Tenochtitlán when we arrived. As soon as the words were out of my mouth, I saw Father looking at me disapprovingly. The captain said, "Perhaps if you're lucky," because Cortés lived in an Aztec palace south of the city in Coyoacán. He added that the child's name was Martin. That was the end of our conversation. From then on, I was enthralled by the idea of meeting Cortés and Marina and seeing the child, Martin.

For the natives, a baby's birth is an omen of change. The villagers celebrated new births, but this one was not celebrated. Strangely, the next day, the villagers remained in their homes; no tortillas were roasting on the fire in the morning.

Chapter 6

The Aztec Shaman

One lazy afternoon, while playing with the village children, I noticed our group getting smaller and smaller. When Tonititu peeled off, he pointed toward a man approaching from the jungle. Within a minute, my sister and I were left standing alone. He came directly towards us. We ran to our house, where Mother and Father sat on a bench with baby Beatriz.

The man was handsome, in his mid-30s, with a medium build and average height. His face was distinguished by his left eyebrow, which was split in two. His bare skin glowed like copper. He wore a loin cloth as was typical of men. A modest cotton cloak was draped over his right shoulder and tied in a knot above his left shoulder. The hair on the top portion of his head was pulled up to the crown and affixed with a blue-green feather comb ornament. The hair below that was pulled back into a thick, tightly twisted long column tied with a cloth bow just below his shoulders. This thick hair almost looked like a dense, narrow black horsehair pillow. He was barefoot.

Father abruptly stood to face this unknown person, shielding Mother and us children. Within speaking distance, the man nodded to signify he was not a threat. The native man, in broken Spanish, introduced himself as Martin Ocelotl. He then shook Father's hand. Father said something in Spanish, which we couldn't hear, but the man appeared to understand. They exchanged a few more words, and at that point, the man reached into a pouch he was carrying. He handed something wrapped in a cloth to Father, and then, with a slight bow, he turned and departed.

We crowded around to see what the man had given him. As he unfolded the cloth, a beautiful solid gold bird emerged. It was about the size of a baby rabbit. Its feathers were etched into the metal with eyes of green jade. Father raised his eyebrows while weighing the bird in his hand, assessing its potential value. He claimed that as soon as we got to Tenochtitlán, he would have it melted down.

Handing Beatriz off to me, Mother interceded. She delicately picked up the exquisite object, proclaiming she would protect it until the time came when a decision was to be made about melting it. She then exchanged the bird for the baby, allowing me to handle it. I thought it was the most beautiful thing I had ever seen. Mother then placed the bird in her bosom, covering it with little Beatrice.

As soon as the man left, Cortés' men rushed over. They told us that the man, Martin Ocelotl, was a pochtecatl (poch te CAT ul), an Aztec trader, and a very wealthy man. He was also a sorcerer or shaman connected with Moctezuma's royal family. To that, Father told the soldiers he had been responsible for finding witches in Spain (in front of me, he never said what he did once they were found). He said men of this kind are evil, and we best distance ourselves from further contact. I didn't know what to think. The man didn't seem menacing to me.

Chapter 7

Onward to Tenochtitlán

Nearing the departure time for Tenochtitlán, Aztec porters were brought in to amass our belongings and provisions in the center of the common area. Most of our goods had been ported to the Aztec capital right after arrival. The captain corralled everyone together to explain the journey ahead. He stated that our trek would take us two hundred miles and two months; we would go the same route Cortés had originally taken. We were told we would be walking; the only exception would be my mother, who would ride one of the men's horses. We were to leave the next day right after sunrise.

Had we been in Spain, we would have gone by carriage. At that point, I realized I had never seen any conveyance with wheels. I suppose it was because there were no real roads, indeed not wide enough for a carriage. Interesting. I observed that everything in this world was carried on the backs of men.

I was surprised when Mother stepped forward, asserting she would need two village women—one to help with us, me and my sister, and one to be a wet nurse for the baby. The captain nodded, saying she should choose whom she wanted, but we were leaving in the morning.

A woman already serving as a wet nurse was selected. The

other one selected was Xitlali. While I was glad she would be coming with us, I hadn't realized she would have to leave her children behind, perhaps indefinitely. I felt awful for my friend Tonititu because he would be losing his mother. At the time, I didn't know that he had already lost his father to smallpox.

We were an entourage of thirty, including soldiers and native porters. When we departed, it was mid-February 1524. After the first two hours, I realized I must have grown because my feet and heels were bleeding from shoes that no longer fit. I knew there were no other shoes for me. When no one was looking, I tossed them down a ravine. Relief! We were required to wear our long skirts again, so no one was the wiser except Xitlali. She, however, gave me a nod of approval.

I remember reaching a high plateau at the end of the first day. The day had been pleasant, even hot, but the night was quite the opposite. It was chilly and windy up there. I appreciated wearing my heavy clothes again, but I could feel them very snug. I had to undo my blouse and skirt's top and bottom buttons. In the evening, by the light of the fire, Father, with his copy of Cortés' *Second Letter*, would describe what we should expect to see in the coming days as we made our way as the conquistadors had. As always, the soldiers made camp each night, and we slept on the ground in rows protected by Cortés' men who stood guard. We were covered with a big tarp to keep the fog that rolled in early morning from settling on us.

By the end of the week, we reached a settlement called Zacatula, which had many adobe houses, much larger than the homes in Huitzilapan. It was evident that smallpox had taken its toll here as well. This town appeared to be a way station accustomed to providing sleeping accommodations for travelers. We were offered a steam bath in one of the large houses. I eagerly took advantage of being able to disrobe and have water poured over me. Mother and Marina were more modest, preferring to wash themselves. Father? No! He asserted that bathing removed the top layer of skin acquired over time, which protected him from infection. He said it had taken him years to develop this barrier, and he was not about to wash it off. Then he asked us if his health was not evidence of its efficacy. A couple of Cortés' men nodded in agreement. One man suggested that Father's stink was a repellant. Everybody laughed. I knew they were laughing at Father. I felt terrible for him, but he stunk.

After several days and sufficient rest, we pressed on to town after town, with strange names. Some towns were more welcoming than others. What fascinated the villagers was me and my sister. We were the first European children the villagers had encountered. There would always be a rush of curious children to see a foreigner their age. I enjoyed their curiosity, but my father disapproved, forbidding me from interacting with them. Sometimes, when Father was not around, I would say something to them in Nahuatl, leaving them stunned.

In the evenings, Cortés' men, with a lot of bravado, would replay the battles they had won at each significant town we passed through. Father would try to identify the passage in Cortés' letter that corresponded to their description.

As we pushed on, by early afternoon, we came upon a ten-foot-high stone wall that stretched from mountain to mountain. Father announced that we must be in Tascalteca (Tlaxcala today). The people there had been enemies of Moctezuma. Three years ago, in Cortés' time, there were 20,000 houses in the city. Cortés described Tascalteca as being like Genoa or Pisa!

One evening, Cortés' men described how Cortés recruited these natives to join him. At first, they said we were in battle with them, but when they realized they would lose, they chose to side with Cortés. They wanted to join Cortés against Moctezuma, their oppressor. Some three thousand of the natives joined Cortes on his march to Tenochtitlán.

I asked for clarification. Did those Aztecs join Cortés? They all turned my way, including Father, whose face had shifted to disapproval. One of the men said that the natives became conquistadors too! I realized I had crossed another invisible line and refrained from further conversation. Father said nothing about the incident, but he watched more closely to ensure I was kept at a distance from the men.

Ahead of us was an ominous volcano the natives called Popocatépetl (Poh-poh-kah-TEH-peh-tl). In Nahuatl, it means "the mountain that smokes." Sometimes, it spewed fumes, rocks, and fire. The natives of our entourage were afraid of an eruption and anxious to move on. So were we!

Our next destination was the city of Cholula. While walking, I could mingle with soldiers more freely because Father was distracted. I felt conflicted. On the one hand, I knew I was being defiant of my father. On the other hand, his restriction did not seem fair. I remember resolving the conflict within myself with the decision to talk with the men while we walked and not to be alone with any one man. One of the soldiers was expounding on the gallantry of Cortés that presaged the overthrow of Moctezuma. His tale was about Doña Marina. My ears perked up. Not only was she named Marina, but she also had the title of Doña! I interjected, asking, "She's Doña like me? Why is that?" The soldier replied that he didn't know why, but that is what Cortés called her. Cortés thought she was exceptional, and so did they, so Doña seemed right.

He continued with his story. When they first got to the city, the priests welcomed them and offered food and accommodations for the Spaniards—but not for the native warriors who had joined them. They said Cortés was suspicious that he surmised it was a plot to corral them and then enslave or murder them, or worse, to deliver them to their emperor, Moctezuma. The soldier related Cortés' strategy. He summoned the Cholula priests to the central square, and once they had assembled, he would fire a single shot into the air. He knew the shot would cause the city's warriors to rush in and investigate. When they did, that was our signal to kill them all. Cortés instructed us to cut off their hands. When we asked why, he told us that Doña Marina said it was necessary. In their culture, according to her, we needed to do that if we wanted them to fear us and be obedient. I had a hard time trying to understand why a woman would propose such brutality. From then on, I also became obsessed with Doña Marina.

From Cholula, our entourage climbed another mountain range until we reached a pass between two more volcanos. Below them, we could see the city of Tenochtitlán. Like the plate in Father's book, the city was situated in the middle of the blue waters of a vast lake. By late afternoon, the blue waters, reflecting the cloudy sky, had turned white as if the city were in the middle of a sea of cotton. It was breathtaking. The conquistadors stood proudly, taking in the distant view.

From our distance, the city looked like a disturbed ant's nest, with streams of worker ants scurrying in long lines. A haze of dust hung over the city. Mother and Father proclaimed it chaos. Mother lamented that the beautiful city Father had described in Cortés' *Letter* was gone. She wanted to know where we were going to live.

From this vantage point, Tenochtitlán was now only a day away. I remember that evening well. I sat on a ledge, looking down at the city. It was chilly. I pulled a blanket around me to keep out the cold. My thoughts shifted to the woman, Doña Marina. I wondered what it would take to be with Cortés and what his palace was like where he lived with her and their son, Martin. Since Father was to be the Treasurer, I wondered if he would be working with Cortés. Realizing I had more questions than answers, I would have to wait. We would be in Tenochtitlán the next day! Would Señor Cordoba be there, I wondered?

Chapter 8
Arrival

The next day, we set out early, with the sun rising behind us, burning off the morning fog and warming their backs. We could hear the sounds coming from the city's reconstruction below. The natives were singing and chanting. It was mesmerizing.

By early afternoon, we arrived at the lake's rim. Despite its glistening appearance from afar, the waters emitted a pungent odor of decaying vegetation. It was very unpleasant. In Spain, we would have days after a rain when the city would stink like that. That smell came from human excrement. We proceeded along the main causeway from land across the water to the city's heart. The distance must have been a mile, at least. It was a more extensive road than any I had seen in Spain and built over the water. Many buildings, probably homes, were set atop hills of earth. It looked like another world.

We passed through a guarded gate, crossed a bridge, and came out onto an expansive street. The street led us to a colossal plaza; I wondered how long it had taken to lay all those stones over such a large area. Everywhere, there were gigantic rubble mounds. Natives were scurrying here and there, sweaty, dirty, laden, and hunched over with sacks of stones slung across their backs, gathered from the mountainous heaps.

Looming before us was the remnant of what used to be the main Aztec pyramid. I remember the image from the picture in Father's book. According to the description in Cortés' *Letter,* sacrificial temples were on the very top. Cortés had razed the temples, and much of the pyramid, but the remaining structure was still impressive. Two giant steps provided the pyramid's base. A pair of parallel stairs led up about fifty feet from that base, where it was effectively chopped off.

As we marveled at the structure, half of Cortés' men departed, their task complete. We were left to rest while the captain of the soldiers sorted out our next steps. By then, the adults seemed engaged in what sounded like an argument. I didn't want any part of that. I scrambled among the heaps of large, shattered stones for a better view and found a path to the steps around the pyramid. From there, I climbed as high as I could. When I looked down, they were all looking up at me. I waved. I could tell they were unhappy and waving for me to come down. From my vantage point, I could see two of the porters making their way up to me. At that point, I realized that my venture was causing a problem and tried to signal that I was coming down. I knew Father was going to be furious with me.

Once I was down, the captain again took charge and

informed us that the others in our group would be taken to live in the former Aztec neighborhood. The Aztecs were forced to abandon their homes and live outside the large island on the mainland. Under Cortés' orders, only Europeans were allowed to live in the city. A couple of the men led them away.

On the other hand, we would be taken to Cortés' palace. I can still hear Father shouting: "What?" He told the captain he would not live under Cortés' roof. The captain explained that it was not a gesture of hospitality but of necessity. All the new high-ranking officials were housed there. Rodrigo Albornoz, the royal accountant, and Diego de Soto, the interim treasurer, stayed there. The captain looked over his shoulder to where the others were headed. To everyone's surprise, Father indicated he would rather live there than be a guest of Cortés. He promptly turned about face to catch up with the others. Mother spoke up, addressing the captain and telling him to let Father go.

The sound of destruction and construction grew. Looking across the plaza, we saw what looked like a heap of dead bodies. Aztec laborers were loading them onto carts and hauling them away. I noted that there were carts with wheels in the city and commented to the captain to that effect. The captain laughed. He told me the Aztecs never discovered the wheel, that they built the whole city without one wheel. The Aztecs were fascinated with many European inventions, especially the wheel. Even the most minor things, like nails, were admired.

A slight breeze picked up the pungent stench. Unfortunately, explained the captain, when Cortés destroyed the Aztec monuments, he also destroyed the infrastructure of canals and freshwater conveyances that kept the city clean and provided fresh water. The reconstruction underway was beginning to repair that. He indicated that the city's reconstruction was moving quickly because there was so much stone they could use from the destroyed pyramid and temples. Dust and noise filled the air. We watched as hundreds of Aztecs dismantled the rubble mounds and moved the rocks to the new church on the plaza's north side.

Cortés' palace was at the southeast corner, just across the bridge. The captain informed us that it used to be one of Moctezuma's palaces, his father's palace, if I remember correctly, that Cortés had co-opted after the conquest. The captain pointed out the *audencia* (court building) on the church's west side on the plaza's far north end, indicating where the Treasury was and where Father was to work.

Ahead of the others, my sister and I scaled the broad steps to the massive front gate of the wall surrounding Cortés' palace. Guards stood at attention. I asked one if this was Cortés' palace. He replied, "Yes," and stamped his sword on the ground to signal we would not be allowed entry.

I turned to watch our entourage approach. They looked tired. When they arrived at the gate, the guard asked which one of us was Alonso de Estrada. Mother and the captain had to explain that he would come in the next few days. Finally, seeing us in our beleaguered condition, they let us in. As we entered, the captain bid us farewell. I was sorry to see him go. He had been more like a father to me than Father had.

Once inside, I was amazed at the high ceilings and wide hallways. The floors were constructed from polished stones. There were beautifully painted walls and scenes of wildlife and trees in the jungle. There were colorful paintings of Aztecs in different costumes, many resembling animals.

We were assigned three adjoining rooms on the second floor, facing a splendid courtyard with an orchard of newly planted apple, pear, and cherry trees. One room was for Mother (and Father), one for Marina and me, and one for baby Beatrice and the wet nurse. The servants hustled Xitlali off to be included as part of the staff. I was impressed. We had beds and candlelight. Mother immediately fell asleep and didn't wake for almost two days.

Chapter 9

Fact versus Rumor

I was determined to discover if the story about Cortés having a pet jaguar was true, so I decided to explore the palace. I realized, by chance, that I might meet Cortés. My current dress would be inappropriate; I looked like a peasant. First, I had to find Xitlali to help me find and go through Mother's clothes chests. Marina was wearing my clothes, but there was nothing more for me.

We did our best. Digging through Mother's clothing chests, we found a skirt, blouse, and vest. Xitlali rolled the skirt and dressed up at the waist to shorten it. She showed me how to keep hold of the roll lest it unravel. Wearing my mother's blouse, I realized I was filling out; my bosom was growing. The vest did an excellent job of hiding my now-thick waist. Shoes? Mother's were still too big. No one could see my feet, so shoes were decided against.

Gripping my waist, I roamed the long corridors, trying every door, curious about what I might find inside. The polished stucco floors were cool to the touch of my bare feet. Further down the corridor, I saw two large doors. I approached and discovered they were unlocked! When I peered inside, it was dark, with only a sliver of light coming from a high-draped window. I entered and crossed the room toward the window, sensing a thick carpet on the floor. I

An RSVP to Hernán Cortés: Doña Luisa de Estrada Tells Her Story

tugged at the drape to reveal the room's contents.

It was an audience room to accommodate perhaps fifty people. Chairs and tables filled the room. Atop each table was a vase of what looked like flowers. Upon closer inspection, I discovered they were not flowers but feathers. As my eyes grew accustomed to the light, the feathers took on spectacular brilliant colors—blue, yellow, turquoise, and red. The chairs were draped with animal skins, shimmering in the dim light. Some were spotted, and others were solid black. I chose a chair with a black pelt. Pulling the chair out from the table, I sat down. As I ran my hands across the shimmering fur, dust particles floated in the air. She reflected on my time in Huitzilapan – the warmth, food, freedom, animals, and people. My native playmate, Tonatiuh, came to mind. I remembered being warned not to venture into the jungle where jaguars roamed.

Suddenly, I was jolted from my daydream by a loud shout from one of the male servants. A jaguar leaped into the room headed for the window, its eyes flashing from the light streaming in. Its fangs glowed white. I jumped up, putting my hands on the arms of the chair. No longer holding my skirts, they unrolled, making a large puddle of material at my feet. I was transfixed in my white pantaloons, now glowing in the dim light. The large cat turned toward me to identify the source of motion. In a split second, it leaped, landing at my feet. The cat's front paws stopped, and its rear legs, unable to stop in time, skidded sideways, almost knocking me over. A young black servant rushed into the room. His eyes were wide with fear. We looked at each other in horror.

The cat snarled and looked up at me. Instinctively, I dared not look directly into its eyes. It was sitting on my feet as if holding me there. I didn't move. Sensing I wasn't going to be mauled or eaten, my whole body relaxed. The cat must have felt my lack of fear; disinterested, it got up and strode out of the room, its shoulders undulating as it walked across the floor. The servant followed, closing the doors behind him. How embarrassing, I thought. Me, standing there in my underwear. Then, I acknowledged out loud that the story about Cortés having a pet jaguar was not a rumor. It was true! No more than ever, I wanted to meet Cortes.

Father arrived refreshed that afternoon and joined the family at the communal dining table. He and Mother appeared to be enjoying their reunion. An Aztec and Spanish meal was laid out before us. Father was satisfied that he could again have his Spanish biscuits and wine. He gorged himself after three months of refusing to eat any native food.

As we sat there, I observed that at least half of the staff were Aztec women in their loose dresses who passed by silently in bare feet. The Spanish staff of men, including three black servants. They clicked and clacked as their heeled shoes struck the stucco floor as they traversed the room.

After our meal, Mother and Father retreated to the courtyard, leaving Marina and me at the grand table, which was now cleared. We watched as servants placed large vases of beautiful flowers on the tables at the room's perimeter. I asked one of the Spanish servants where all the flowers had come from. He replied that there was an island south of the city, not too far, where all the flowers were grown. Cortés had preserved it from destruction because of its beauty. I wanted to go and see it.

The flowers and the flower island only intensified my fascination with Cortés. He seemed all-powerful. He protected my family, provided for them, had the only palace, and was building a church. But most noteworthy was that he was the famous conquistador who conquered the Aztecs. He destroyed their temples and prevented sacrifices. He did, indeed, have a pet jaguar. Only kings could do something like that, I thought.

Chapter 10

A Moment of Freedom

I expected Señor Cordoba to appear at the palace and ask for me. When that didn't happen, I anxiously waited for his communication, asking Father daily if there was a letter for me. I concluded he must still be in Cuba or dead. Surely, he would write if he could; if he couldn't, what could be the reason other than death?

There wasn't much for my sister or me to do all day in the palace. We weren't allowed out alone; there was nowhere to go. We spent most of our time in the courtyard or the audience room at a table with a book. The vases of feathers no longer held their allure, but I always chose my seat with the black jaguar pelt.

Like our family, Rodrigo de Albornoz and his family stayed at Cortés' palace while their home was being built. Albornoz was appointed to serve alongside Father as an auditor of the Treasury. He had arrived several months before us with his wife, two children, and a niece. With so many of us staying at the palace, which had become more like a boarding house, the only way to accommodate our meals was to set up two communal seatings, one in the morning and one in the late afternoon, in a large banquet room.

Our family and the Albornoz family chose the four-thirty seating. One afternoon, over our meal, Mother approached Señora

Carolina, Albornoz's wife, about a mutually beneficial arrangement. I listened as Mother asked if their son and niece could tutor Marina and me. Their son, Diego, was twenty-one years old and skilled in math, accounting, history, and French. Isabel, their niece, was nineteen. She was married, waiting for her husband, a conquistador, to return from a campaign to the south. She was trained in music, dancing, and embroidery.

I watched as Señora Carolina leaned into Mother, commenting: "Idle hands were the work of the devil." I thought she was referring to me and my sister. I felt embarrassed. Had I made a nuisance of myself? When I asked Mother about it later, she said that Señora Carolina was concerned that her son and niece were spending too much time together, unattended. She assured me that Marina and I were perfectly well-behaved children. When I heard her referring to me as a child, I felt my sense of self and independence arise; I was turning into a young lady. It was then that I decided to tell my mother about Señor Cordoba.

Mother suggested that we move to the courtyard where Beatrice was being taken care of by a nanny, a young woman who had arrived from Spain only to find her husband had been killed. As we walked outside, she took my hand and pulled me close. We found a bench under an arbor that provided us with some shade. To my surprise, she asked if my daily question to my father about an expected letter had something to do with my anxiety. Not much gets past my mother! I confessed my longing for Señor Cordoba, that we had exchanged letters, and that I expected him to be in the colony last August, but sadly, I had not heard from him since our arrival.

With my head on her shoulder, looking out into the courtyard, I waited for her to say something, but she stayed silent. Finally, she told me she knew Luis was going to the New World, seeking adventure; he had told her of his plans. And then what she told me clarified everything–after I understood it. Luis Cordoba, said Mother, was a charming, intelligent man and tutor who favored other men romantically. I hadn't understood what she meant at first. In my mind, I replayed what she said: Romantically. I asked. Romantically? She confirmed. I thought back to that day he told us he was leaving. I remembered how fond he was of my brother and their special friendship and how cautious he seemed with me. I thought I understood what she meant at the time.

Our formal education was to begin again next week. We had our two tutors and a palace room in the back corner of the second floor. It had been a storeroom of jumbled Aztec artifacts that was cleared and cleaned. It was long and narrow, with a high window at the end. That end was set up with tables and chairs for instruction because of the natural light in the morning. The other end near the door was used for music and dance. By the time the adults had scrounged for materials and books, pilfering paper and writing supplies from the *audencia*, three other children ranging in age from eight to thirteen had joined us. We were now a group of seven: The Albornoz's younger son, who was seven years old; an eight-year-old girl; a thirteen-year-old boy, Marina and me, plus the two tutors.

I was delighted. Señor Diego Albornoz was much like my older brother, Luis Alfonso, but more handsome and beguiling. As for Señora Isabel, I wasn't quite so sure. There was something about her, something off. I decided to wait and see until I got to know her better. Since Mother informed me there was a concern about too much familiarity between them, I watched for any untoward behavior.

My sister, Marina, quickly became friends with the young ones. I had more of an affinity with the thirteen-year-old boy, Francisco. He was intelligent and funny but a bit shy. I wasn't sure how he came to be in the palace since his parents were never sighted.

Tutoring sessions lasted from about ten in the morning until noon. Mathematics and geography were always first. Señor Diego's knowledge was hardly comparable to Señor Cordoba's. In all fairness, I made allowances for the fact that he was not a "real" tutor. There was a siesta in the middle of the day until two thirty. Reading, writing, history, or French took up the afternoons until four-thirty. On Fridays, there would be dance instruction and singing. Without music to dance to, we followed Isabel, who conducted our movements as if we were all deaf. Singing was always a favorite;

Isabel had the most beautiful voice and a gift for teaching harmony. We mainly sang Christian hymns. Managing that age range of children would have been a challenge for even a trained teacher. Most of the guests welcomed the structured gaiety of the children.

It was July, and with it, torrential rains. Reconstruction projects in the city were halted; there was no way to work in those conditions. It was just after siesta time, midday. We students collected in the study room, ready to start the afternoon lessons, but our tutors were absent. Above us, the rain pounded on the roof until it suddenly stopped. It was a moment of freedom from supervision. I took the lead and led the others down the back stairs-- quietly so as not to wake late siesta risers. Then, out of the palace, we made our way to the back gate of the enclosure surrounding the building. I don't know where the guard who usually stood there was. No matter. We made our way along the wall until we reached the corner at the front of the palace. Before us was the vast glistening stone plaza; a steamy mist rose from its surface. The quiet created an eerie mixed sensation of solitude and triumph. Francisco and I stood there. Before us was our new world, our future.

The little ones wanted to return, complaining they were cold and wet. I wanted to enter the plaza and spin around until I was dizzy. Marina tugged at my dress, begging me to go back in. Knowing we would be missed, and the tutors should have discovered us gone by now, I led us back, sloshing in mud that had formed around the perimeter.

Right after entering the door to go up the back stairs, I hushed the young ones and instructed them to take off their shoes and stockings like I was doing and leave them neatly lined up against the wall. The girls' skirts, albeit rimmed with a hem of mud, would cover their bare feet, a trick I learned on my trek to Tenochtitlán. The boys. That was a problem. There they stood on their bare, skinny legs and bony knees, shivering. Francisco said he would sneak up to his room, get dry clothes, and meet me in the classroom. That left the Albornoz boy. We had no time left and had to make it up the stairs. I wasn't sure what I would do if we were caught.

I was in luck. Coming down the stairs was Xitlali, who surveyed the situation and saw all the shoes and stockings along the wall. I handed off the Albornoz boy, knowing that Xitlali would find his caretakers. I felt a little guilty and wondered what story Xitlali would make up to explain his barefoot condition. I also wondered what he would say to explain himself.

When we reconvened in the classroom, the tutors were there, elbow to elbow, absorbed in a book. Francisco walked in as if nothing had happened and gave me a wink. I gave Marina a look to indicate nothing should be said, a message she conveyed to her friend. The Albornoz boy never appeared. That day was a new beginning for me. My feelings for Luis Cordoba no longer chained my heart.

Chapter 11

A Bargain with the Devil

Father was grumpy as usual as we sat as a family for our afternoon meal. He poked and prodded at his food and mumbled under his breath. I stayed silent, not wanting to get barked at. I observed Mother approach Father by asking him about work at the *audencia* that morning. That was enough to uncap Father's frustration. He complained of constant infighting between him, Albornoz, and Zuazo in the audencia. He said Zuazo did all of Cortés' bidding, expecting Father to abide by his decrees. It seemed they couldn't agree on anything. Their latest disagreement was over salt. Father said the colony was about to erupt into chaos, all because of Cortés.

He explained that Cortés was so concerned with completing as much reconstruction as quickly as possible that he hadn't released the natives for the two past dry seasons when they shifted their labor to salt extraction. Consequently, salt was in short supply, and the commodity's price was causing unrest. According to the records in the *audiencia*, the Aztecs used more than 20,000 tons of salt a year. Since colonization, taxes on salt added a significant amount of income to the treasury. And now there was a shortage.

Then Father told us that Martin Ocelotl appeared in the *audencia* that morning and requested to see him, saying he had a solution to the salt shortage. Mother and I shared a knowing glance in recognition of the Aztec man who had visited us in Huitzilapan. Mother, trying her best to be supportive, asked what Ocelotl had proposed. Father said that Martin (Father emphasized his Christian name) explained that the Aztecs were agitated because an Aztec festival that honored the fertility goddess (Huixlochihuat), who presided over salt and salt water, was coming up, making them acutely aware of the salt shortage and the cost of salt.

Father said Martin dared to bargain with him over salt. Hanging his head low, Father explained that he had no choice but to agree to his terms. Mother had to ask what the bargain was. According to Father, Ocelotl had warehouses full of salt that he was willing to sell, but he would not sell it unless he didn't have to pay taxes. Father looked at Mother and asked her what she thought he should have done.

At this point, Mother did not ask another question but sat and listened. There was an uncomfortable pause, and then Father added that there was an upside to the bargain. If he agreed with Martin's deal, he would retire from trading; the salt bargain would be his last. Father declared he had done the deal, saying that would be the last of Ocelotl.

Having confessed his bargain with the devil, as he described it, Father put down his fork and shoved his plate away. He said he needed to get back to the *audencia*; there was more trouble brewing because of Cortés. He said that because Cortés was leaving for Honduras, he had appointed him, Rodrigo Albornoz, and Alonso de Zuazo as triumvirates in charge of the government.

I thought I heard right. My father was not only the Treasurer but also the Governor—a Governor-- standing in for Cortés! It was the highest post in the colony! But alas, the sad news was that Cortés was leaving, and I still had not met my idol.

Chapter 12

A Revelation

A frequent visitor at Cortés palace was a man named Alonso García Bravo. He was the city's planner and civil employee of Cortés. He oversaw Tenochtitlán's reconstruction, ensuring it was modeled after a traditional Spanish town, oriented north-south, with a plaza in the middle and a church on the plaza's north side. Aztec Tenochtitlán was oriented just the opposite, east-west.

My father, mother, Rodrigo Albornoz, and his wife would meet García Bravo on Wednesday afternoons right after mealtime to get updates on the construction of our homes. On one of those occasions, I happened to be present. Not wanting to be shooed away by Father, I sat quietly, hoping not to be noticed.

García Bravo arrived and immediately put everyone at ease. He was intelligent, witty, and insightful, yet respectful of his superiors. I was surprised he knew everything in the colony, even Father's bargain with Ocelotl. He made a sideways comment that Ocelotl, the trader, was now Ocelotl the Shaman, who was currently in Tenochtitlán tending to a high-ranking Aztec who had fallen ill. He was crafty with his language and quickly moved on to other topics, not giving Father a chance to say anything.

He was average height, slender, plainly dressed, and already balding in his mid-thirties. From what I could tell, he was not married. I took an instant liking to him. After updating the Albornozes on their home and informing Mother and Father about theirs, Father indicated he was too occupied with the *audencia*, that from now on, he would leave all construction decisions up to Mother.

After their meeting, I told Mother I would like to take my father's place and report on the progress of our home. She readily agreed, knowing that García Bravo was trustworthy and would, as always, be reporting to her weekly.

There was a unique bond between me and García Bravo. He was not a father figure but more like a benevolent uncle, a confidant, a teacher. I adored him. He treated me like an equal and explained construction details, surveying, drafting, and problems with the Aztec labor. But what fascinated me most was his profound knowledge of the Aztecs and their culture.

We spent days together. It was a conflict for Mother, who preferred that I attend tutoring sessions, but she knew the value of my relationship with García Bravo. Wherever we went, we gathered a small crowd hoping to learn the latest gossip about which conquistador would be building a palace or which conquistador had taken up with an Aztec woman. García Bravo knew who was new to the colony and the resources they brought with them. In the evenings, we would attend parties together. Mother considered him my chaperone. Father paid little attention, caught up in politics at the audencia.

Our visits to our home –really a palace as befits a Governor-- were always an astonishing experience. With almost around-the-clock construction, it rose amazingly fast; each visit revealed new walls, rooms, and possibilities. It was only two stories. I asked García Bravo why it didn't have more levels. That was Cortés's doing, he said, for two reasons. Both had to do with the cost of reconstruction. Tenochtitlán was built in the middle of the lake, and buildings slowly sank. When a building sank, at a certain point, it essentially crumbled in on itself. The second was because of earthquakes. Amere rumbling could destroy a building. My thoughts were that Cortés must be one of the wisest men alive.

Mother got involved with the finer details of the construction of our palace and worked with Fray Pedro de Gante. Across the plaza to the west, the Frays' mission was being built on the grounds of Moctezuma's former gardens. With that construction, the plants and trees that needed to be removed were transplanted to our palace. Aztecs who had worked in Moctezuma's gardens were enlisted to create ours. Inside, Aztec artists were painting the walls of the grand ballroom. The walls were covered with frescoes depicting the lush Aztec forests. It reminded me of Huitzilapan. There were vibrant birds, majestic jaguars, and playful monkeys. Even the ceiling was

An RSVP to Hernán Cortés: Doña Luisa de Estrada Tells Her Story

a work of art, painted to resemble the sky with clouds scudding by. There was a striking image of Popocatépetl, the volcano that marks everyone's journey to Tenochtitlán.

Late one afternoon, we sat on a pile of stones in the garden, admiring its emerging beauty. The Aztec labor had been called to another job that day. Because of our closeness, he had listened to me idolizing the conquistador Cortés for months. He hadn't said much, probably because he depended on Cortés for his position. I realized I had been prattling along and looked up to see García Bravo staring intently at me. When I asked, "What?" He said he would tell me something about Cortés that might change my mind. I was intrigued.

He informed me that almost two years ago, Cortés' first wife, Catalina, from Cuba, had come to be with him. She had arrived uninvited. When she didn't find him in Tenochtitlán, she went to his palace in Coyoacán. She found him with Doña Marina and their son, Martin, just one year old. Several Aztec women were also living with them. Apparently, she did not like what she saw. Surprised by her visit, Cortés held a party in her honor, and the guests were treated to food and wine. With too much to drink, Cortés flirted with several women. Catalina objected, and they started to argue. The argument escalated, and they went upstairs to her room. According to the servants, there was more shouting and a loud crash as something fell on the floor. When they rushed in, Catalina was on the floor with Cortés over her body, pearls strewn everywhere. The servants said they saw scratch marks on his face. When Cortés looked up, he claimed he was only trying to help her, that she had had an asthma attack. At the inquisition into Catalina's death, no one would say anything against Cortés. He was found not guilty of murder.

That story about Cortés did give me pause. I had seen my parents argue, but I could not imagine my father throttling my mother. I decided then and there to sequester my adoration for the Conquistador. García Bravo had done me a favor.

Chapter 13

An Aztec Sacrifice

It was early morning, and Mother said she would be at the *audencia* all day to discuss financing the building of several shops on the plaza's west side. Mother was also going to build a grist mill on the edge of town to produce flour for the favored biscuits of the Spanish. García Bravo had advised them that it would be a good investment.

Since my father was a salaried civil servant and paid very well, that was his only source of income. The shops and grist mill would make up for the fact that he had no rights to land and labor, called an *encomienda*, the path to riches in New Spain. Cortés gave those grants to his relatives and conquistador friends. Father was incensed about that. He said would ask García Bravo why the King didn't stop Cortés since it enhanced his power and influence, which is precisely what the King was concerned about.

There was no tutoring that day, so my sister and I were left in Xitlali's care, who suggested she would take us to Xochimilco (So chi MIL co), the flower market. I had looked forward to going there since I was informed that this was where the flowers for Cortés' palace were grown.

After Mother's carriage ferried her off to the plaza's north side, we left, headed in the opposite direction, south, to catch a gondola that would take us through a canal into another lake, Lake Xochimilco.

Along the way, Xitlali bought us food from a local native vendor. I loved it; it reminded me of our time in Huitilapan. Marina ate hers only because she was hungry. As usual, we got stared at because we were Spanish children, which is still a rarity. There were natives everywhere. That day was an Aztec celebration, and the natives were adorned with brightly colored feathers and carrying decorated cloth banners. Xitlali told us that the Aztecs were celebrating the Sun God, Huitzilopochtli. (wit zil o POCH til lee). Our gondola was a little boat with benches covered by a cloth roof of brightly colored fabric. It was very festive.

Once we reached a small island and left our small boat so it could return for more riders, we became aware of the crowd surrounding us. I felt like a fish in a big school of fish, like I had seen on our voyage to the New World. Everyone turned in unison this way and that.

Then I heard drums. Xitlali grabbed our hands, holding them tight, and pulled us close to her. She said something in Nahuatl that I could not understand, but intuitively, I knew I must stay with her. The drums in the background dictated the pace of the crowd. I became aware of my heart pounding in my chest. It wasn't fear that I felt, but excitement.

A dust cloud formed above the swarm of people and hovered magically over us, illuminated by the afternoon sun. As we moved forward, the drums got louder and louder. I could feel the ambient pressure of sweaty bodies surrounding me. Children were held closely by their parents. Suddenly, the drums ceased, and the crowd came to a halt. There was no silence.

All eyes looked up, fixated on five Aztec Priests in black robes, blackened faces, and matted straggly hair. The priests stood on an elevated platform upon which a large wooden plank altar was topped with a large boulder.

The drums resumed their beating, this time in a steady roll. The crowd's murmuring grew louder until the screams of a young boy, not much older than me, broke above the din. Again, the crowd hushed. The priests, each holding an arm or leg, lifted the terrified boy onto the altar, his back arched over the rock, his head hanging down. The boy struggled, but the priest held him down.

Not knowing what would come, I watched in amazement as the priest magically lifted the boy's beating heart out of his chest and raised it to the sky. Blood streamed down his arms and gushed from the boy's body. His blood was caught in bowls placed beneath the altar. The priest uttered something in Aztec that I could not understand. The crowd resounded in shouts of approval, moving like a wave to and fro.

Xitlali pulled us sideways through the crowd, weaving in and out until we came to a vacant, lonely street littered with feathers and trampled flowers. As we stood there, Xitlali, holding our hands tight, looked to the sky and chanted, "Now, the sun will keep moving across the skies, and darkness will not overcome us. Our people will live on. God, Huitzilopochtli has been fed. "

My sister and I were mesmerized. Xitlali seemed like a different person. I would have to ask her later to translate.

Xitlali led us back to where we could catch a boat back to Tenochtitlán. The roar from the crowd could again be heard growing louder and louder. Several oarsmen for the boats arrived, surprised to find us there. We were quickly herded into a gondola. The ride was silent as the oars speedily but quietly and rhythmically bore us across the water. I replayed the scene of the sacrifice over and over in my mind. I looked at Xitlali to see that she returned to her usual self.

As each stroke of the boatman's oar propelled us back, I reflected on what I knew about the Aztecs. Cortés banned these sacrifices. I wondered why this one had taken place. I thought that Xitlali must have known what would happen that day. I also felt that she was more native than I realized.

Returning to the palace was quite different. The plaza was essentially deserted, and it was obvious that the Aztecs were still in

Xochimilco for the festivities. On our way to the palace, we observed a group of settlers surrounding a Franciscan Fray. They seemed agitated about something. Then, one of them, who looked like one of Father's judges, turned and ran north towards the *audencia*. Oh no, I thought. They were probably telling the Fray about the sacrifice in Xochimilco.

When we arrived at the palace, Marina and I went up to the classroom to see if we could find something to read. A servant came to fetch us for dinner. Mother, Father, and García Bravo were engaged in conversation. Around us, chatter intensified. The sacrifice in Xochimilco was THE topic of discussion. We said nothing.

Chapter 14

Chaos & Suspicions

Our palace was finally finished. I was saddened that my days with García Bravo dwindled as he focused on other construction projects. Furnishings were sparse, but we had beds, and the parlor had enough furniture to entertain at least eight guests. The dining room was furnished with three small tables end to end that could seat fourteen. Father's family members and servants who resided in Santiago, Cuba, were sent for. They would move in with us until suitable housing could be secured. The household was coming together. Father found some solace now that we were out of Cortés' palace. He focused on the attached stables, where he kept several horses and his private carriage.

Father came bounding in the front door on a drab day in December. He hadn't gone to the stables first, as usual. He was shouting at the top of his lungs, alarming everyone who rushed to see what the commotion was all about. Mother and I were working on some accounting books, and we dropped everything and dashed downstairs.

Father roared. Cortés was interfering with HIS government again. Gonzalo Salazar and Pedro Almíndez had returned from Honduras, where they had gone as Cortés' chaperones because the

King decided Cortés needed watching. They arrived in the afternoon waving a decree signed by Cortés, allowing, NO, usurping control of the government from him. Cortés' supporter, Zuazo, was allowed to stay in power, but Albornoz and Father were ousted. He shouted that Cortés was up to something. He said he was afraid of being arrested, so he came home to save himself and protect us. He ordered all the servants to be on the lookout for unusual activity and not to allow anyone into the palace.

Later, over dinner, Father said Salazar was the man he feared most. He could take over the Treasury since that was his profession. Another critical factor was that he was responsible for the colony's arms and ammunition. He asked Mother if perhaps they were planning a coup. Of course, she had no way to answer.

Father dismissed himself, saying he needed to write a letter to the Crown informing the King of the latest developments. The reality was stark—a response could take until almost May: two months for his letter to reach its destination and another two months for a reply, at best.

Weeks passed, and Father never left the house. Alonso García Bravo and Rodrigo Albornoz spent much of their day sequestered in the parlor with Father, strategizing how to deal with the disastrous situation. It was García Bravo, in tune with the underbelly of the colony, who broke the news that Salazar and

Chirino had duped everyone. There had been two decrees from Cortés; they had hidden the first. The first decree stipulated that Salazar and Chirino would join, not replace Father and Albornoz, and form a group of five. Father was outraged, but without the King behind him, he had no power to challenge the usurpers.

Father's lawyers got involved, and by February, Father, and Albornoz were reinstated by nullifying the second decree and enacting the first. But, instead of every group member having equal power, Father and Albornoz were ranked below Salazar and Chirino. Father was incensed.

By April 1525, the situation worsened. Salazar and Chirino reasserted themselves; they proclaimed that anyone who recognized Father and Albornoz would face one hundred lashes and the confiscation of their property. Even Zuazo signed their proclamation.

The worst news soon arrived. Salazar and Chirino said they had news that Cortés and his conquistadors were killed in Honduras. That day was the worst for me. I was never going to meet Cortés. It was also the worst day for Albornoz. He and his whole family, including his youngest son, Diego, our tutor, and Isabel, his niece, our other tutor, showed up at our palace, seeking refuge. They had fled Cortés' palace as Salazar and Chirino took it over.

Throughout the day, many of Cortés' palace residents

begged Father to let them in. Our palace was full. Each room was crowded with four, five, or six people. Our problem was food! It seemed we were being held hostage in our own home. Father was most worried about the stables and his horses. He warned us he needed to escape or face arrest. We were in the worst state of anguish when he and Albornoz, atop Father's best horses, raced out the palace gate before dawn the following day.

Again, García Bravo was our link to what was happening in the colony and government. He told us that Zuazo had fled to Cuba. Salazar and Chirino were in the process of confiscating Cortés' properties and arresting Cortés supporters. They had surrounded Cortés' palace with cannons, daring anyone to try and take it from them.

Just after sunrise the next day, representatives from the seized government came to our palace to inform us that Father had been captured and taken prisoner. With that news, Mother, fearing for our safety, ordered me to find Xitlali, who was not living with us and all the Albornozes, and meet in her chamber on the second floor, the furthest from the palace's entry. I dashed about, looking for them, and found Diego and Isabel; to their surprise, I ordered them to Mother's chamber. Along the way, I found Xitlali. She went searching for Señor and Señora Albornoz and their youngest son.

Once we were inside, we set about barricading ourselves in.

With no way to bolt the doors, Señor Diego tried in vain to tie them shut with sashes through the door's heavy brass handles. The fabric quickly unraveled. Seeing this futile endeavor, I intervened. I ordered them to strip the sheets from the bed and tear them into strips. Tugging at the sheets that would not yield to a tear, Señora Isabel produced a pair of embroidery scissors. From the strips, Marina and I used our skills to make braids.

I took the braids, put them through the door handles, and tied a bowline knot, securely fastening the door. When Señor Diego asked me how I knew how to tie knots, I told him Gilberto from our caravel had taught me. We waited in the dark, people strewn on the bed and carpets, not wanting Salazar or Chirino's men to see a flicker of light from the high window of Mother's chamber.

The following day, García Bravo arrived to check on us. He was surprised to learn we were barricaded in. Not wanting to alarm us, he knocked on the door and identified himself.

My ears perked immediately, and I rushed to untie the rope but stopped. I asked if we were safe and if he was alone, afraid that he might be there against his will or the pawn of some trick by Salazar to get us to open the door. I asked him a question about me that I knew only he would know the answer to. If he gave me the wrong answer, it would be a tip-off that he was not free. I asked him, "Who is the Pequeña Sirena?" When he answered that it was me, I knew it was safe to open the door. Everyone in the room was bewildered.

Once the doors were opened, García Bravo assured them they were safe. I ran to his embrace, and the others went downstairs, famished after the long night. At Mother's suggestion, we reconvened in the parlor so García Bravo could report what was happening in the colony.

Chapter 15

Cortés is Alive

García Bravo told us that the colony was in a state of lawlessness. My father was being held as a prisoner but was otherwise fine; his lawyers are working on his release. Zuazo had made it safely to Cuba. For the time being, Salazar was focused on securing his position as head of the government. We are waiting for the King to intercede.

After several weeks, my father was released under house arrest, but at least he was free. One morning, García Bravo arrived very early. We were not dressed yet, but as a frequent visitor to our palace, the servants knew to let him in. They led him to the parlor to wait for Father. I heard my parents getting dressed, and I readied myself, following them down the stairs to the parlor.

When we entered, his first words were: "Cortés is alive!" My jaw must have dropped. Alive? I was conflicted. On the one hand, I was elated and anxious to meet him, finally. On the other hand, what he had done to Father, and of course, the case against him for murdering his wife, checked my enthusiasm.

Father was suspicious. García Bravo explained that he had seen a hand-delivered letter from Cortés' page stating he was very much alive. He said that Zuazo, in Cuba, had received a letter from

Cortés requesting supplies be sent to Honduras. Zuazo had written back and informed him of the situation in the colony, and Cortés confirmed that he was not dead.

Father asked if Cortés had said anything else in his letter. García replied that Cortés had written that Francisco de las Casa, his cousin who had gone with him to Honduras, should replace Salazar and Chirino.

Father was furious, stating that an almost dead man, off in Honduras, was still dictating terms in the colony. Of course, neither Father nor García Bravo believed those two men would give up their power. Also in the letter, Cortés wrote that he wanted my father to organize supporters, naming him lieutenant governor. Father asked García Bravo if that sounded like an impending war. We were put on high alert again, and our palace was turned into a fortress.

Weeks later, when Francisco de las Casa showed up at the *audencia* to claim government control, Salazar and Chirino had him arrested, put on a ship, and sent to Spain as a prisoner.

We waited. Father, Albornoz, García Bravo, and several other high-ranking aristocrats spent hours behind closed doors in our parlor. They were planning something.

My father took the lead and gathered a group of Cortés supporters. They armed themselves as best they could and attacked Salazar in Cortés' palace. According to my father's telling of this maneuver, when they showed up, Salazar's men fled. They were able to capture and imprison Salazar. Chirino fled, but they caught him, too. García Bravo said my father was a hero!

But his exalted status did not last long. What happened next, in my opinion, disgraced my family. My mother and I, as well as García Bravo, couldn't believe what we heard. When Father and Albornoz assumed government control, they initiated legal proceedings against Salazar and Chirino. But, to the colony's shock, disappointment, and disapproval, they set out to seek revenge. They arrested some of Salazar and Chirino's supporters, executing them. Then, like their former enemies, they seized property for themselves. According to García Bravo, Father re-assigned one of Cortés' largest encomienda estates, with the highest number of laborers and, consequently, the highest profit, to himself.

Mother and I were appalled. Undoubtedly, the King would eventually find out. For now, with all the civil servants in the *audencia*, someone would leak that information to the citizenry. I wondered if all of us would be vilified because of Father's deeds.

Chapter 16

Cortés Returns from Honduras

The comings and goings at our palace were constant. Father summoned his supporters, many of whom were living with us, to announce that the King had finally intervened. It wasn't what he expected, but at least they had the King's attention. Father and Diego Albornoz were going to be replaced by a man named Luis Ponce de Leon. He would be arriving soon.

I was elated. Father as governor was, in my mind, a disaster. I was still considered a child, but I had ears, and the stories of Father's greediness kept me from making friends as people shied away from the social events I attended. García Bravo did his best to support Father, but I could tell he disapproved of his actions.

Ponce de Leon didn't arrive for many months. When he finally arrived, it was May. He was invited to stay at our palace, preferring not to stay at Cortés'. To everyone's surprise, Cortés arrived from Honduras about the same time, moving back into this ransacked palace. All anyone could talk about was the impending dynamic between Father, Albornoz, Ponce de Leon, and Cortés.

The next thing I knew was that we received an invitation to Cortés' palace for a dinner in honor of Ponce de Leon. Finally, I was going to meet Cortés! I had been waiting for this moment for three years. I was now thirteen.

It was as much a welcome home banquet for Cortés as a banquet in honor of Ponce de Leon's arrival and appointment as governor. The tables were set with beautiful flowers and elegant silver candelabras. Cortés showed off by having all his black servants attend to the guests, including the one I met, who had come to my rescue in the audience room with the jaguar.

At the banquet's start, Cortés seemed quite boastful, but I found him quite affable; he charmed the guests, making them laugh several times. His biggest joke, of course, was that he was still alive! He was a handsome man in his early forties. I could see why the ladies liked him so much. He seemed very "Kingly." In contrast, Father looked so much older. He was almost sixty.

Sitting across the table from my family were the famous Alvarado brothers: Jorge, Gómez, and Juan. The eldest brother, infamous Pedro, considered Cortés' right-hand man, was not in attendance. He was on another conquest mission in Guatemala. The brothers were known as "First Conquerors," the conquistadors who had been with Cortés when they won the battle for Tenochtitlán. Another notable guest was First Conqueror, Gonzalo de Sandoval. In the years since, many had become rich after Cortés rewarded them with *encomiendas* of land and labor. . Their palaces sprang up in the city's core, one after the other. Each one was trying to outdo the other in splendor. I knew all of this because of García Bravo.

Over dinner, Jorge Alvarado and I locked eyes; it was love at first sight for me. I could feel my body flush with excitement. When I dropped my fork, it tipped over my wine glass. Everyone seemed to be looking at me. I wondered if they could see how red my cheeks were. This feeling was nothing like the feelings I had had for Señor Cordoba.

When Cortés introduced Jorge to the guests and asked him to say a few words, he blushed! I knew it was because of me. His comments were sincere. He said something about what a beautiful world they were living in and what intelligent people the Aztecs were. His short speech was a blur. I might have fainted until I was brought back to reality with the realization that Mother's hand was giving me a knowing caress. As for Cortés? All I could think of was Jorge.

Within days of the banquet, the announcement came that Ponce de Leon was dead, found on a bench in the plaza. Rumors swirled that Cortés had something to do with it. Perhaps it was poison. I reflected on the banquet, asking myself how could Cortés have poisoned Ponce de Leon with so many people around? I remembered saying good night to Señor de Leon. He seemed fine. He had given me a slight bow, kissed my hand, and then said good night to Mother and Father. Maybe Cortés had a hand in their deaths, but I didn't know how. What exactly happened that night? I asked myself. My answer was: "That's the night I met Jorge!"

Ponce de Leon had named Marco de Aguilar as his successor should something happen to him. The two had arrived together. Within a month of Ponce de Leon's death, he, too, was dead. It was February of 1527. Father became governor again, but not alone.

Chapter 17

A Discovery

Mother had come to New Spain with plans to expand her family's very successful import/export business. In the colony, she discovered a high demand for European goods from the wealthy.

Despite all the boarders at our palace, Mother continued with the furnishings and décor. As a merchant, she had the finest carved wood tables, many with intricate parquetry, chairs, sofas, thick wool carpets, and elegant damask window draperies, most from Spain but also Italy and France.

It was late afternoon. The drapes were partially pulled, darkening the salon where Mother conducted her private affairs. As I passed Mother's room, I observed her from the doorway. She was inspecting a new piece of furniture. It was a large *vargueno* (what we call a secretary today). I stopped and watched as she checked all the side drawers to see if they opened and closed smoothly. Her fingers coursed over the beautiful parquetry of the polished oak wood. She opened the front to let down the writing surface and displayed the inside of cubbies and drawers. She pulled out a letter and three keys from a top drawer.

She drew the heavy drapes ajar, letting in more light. Then, she dragged a walnut and red velvet upholstered armchair across the carpet to the desk and sat down. She unfolded the letter and read it aloud.

> My cherished daughter, we miss you. The news about the colony is both exciting and alarming. We cannot imagine how you can live among those savages.
>
> The description of your palace is surprising; its construction has been so fast. Indeed, the architects and builders there are doing a tremendous job creating a New Spain with many palaces. The increased shipping business is welcomed. Despite the exorbitant prices you are charging, it seems there is no end to the demand for European goods there.
>
> I will not give you a long account of all the changes here on the continent, as I believe these will pale when compared to the changes where you are. Suffice it to say that the world is changing.
>
> We do not have the same access to the Crown as in Isabella's time. King Charles can never seem to make up his mind. He spends and spends with the idea that the New World will bring him the riches to replenish the treasury. Enough with that, we say.
>
> The varqueño is from Queen Isabella's court. We managed to acquire it through family connections. Inside, you will find the item you requested. I trust that everything is to your satisfaction.
>
> Your children, Luis Alfonso and Ana, are doing well. I receive updates on their welfare every three months. The support Alonso sent on their behalf is more than adequate.
>
> We were pleased to hear about your choice

for Luisa's engagement. The Alvarado family is well respected and known for their sons' conquest activities in the New World.

Give my greetings to Alonso. Congratulations on your new business adventure. I am sure the grist mill will do well.

No more, my dear. May our Lord keep you in his hand for me.

--Mother

I was dumbfounded. Had I heard what I thought I heard? My engagement to Jorge Alvarado? The idea of a future marriage set my head spinning. Yes, I was coming of age! Yes, Mother saw my ardor for him at the dinner for Ponce de Leon.

My attention was drawn again to Mother. *Vargueños*, like this one, are known for their secret compartments. She pushed and pulled each opening, feeling with the tips of her fingers for hidden triggers that would release a segment. Ah ha! She found it above a drawer on the right side. Mother then pulled the entire section out. I watched as an exquisite silver menorah was extracted from its hiding place. Why did my mother have a menorah, I wondered?

I started to enter the room but stopped when I heard Mother say something that sounded like a prayer but was not in Spanish. At this point, I was shivering with anxiety, not understanding what had happened.

Mother caught sight of me as she started to put the menorah back into the desk. I could tell from the look on her face she knew what I had seen and heard. Calmly, she told me to lock the door and pull up another chair. When I was seated, she handed the menorah to me. I set the object in my lap rather than inspecting it and looked up at her, bursting out with a barrage of questions asking her if she was a Crypto-Jew, if she wasn't afraid of the Inquisition, and if Father knew.

My mother said the menorah is a family heirloom handed down from generation to generation. Then she responded with an explanation I never expected. She said that, yes, it means she is Jewish. I felt my eyes flutter with disbelief, thinking if she was Jewish, then obviously I was Jewish. I couldn't respond. My mind raced from thought to thought, each with worse implications: She could be charged with blasphemy by the church, hanged, publicly humiliated, —and so forth.

Mother pulled her chair closer and continued. Her family had converted to Christianity many, many, many years ago (note she did not say how many years ago). Her family had kept the menorah to remind them of their past. She said she could remember seeing it when she was about my age and that her mother had also kept it hidden. She asked me if I had ever wondered why she called my little sister Mi Dulce. I hadn't. She explained that Dulce, which means sweet, is a common name for girls in the Jewish culture. It

An RSVP to Hernán Cortés: Doña Luisa de Estrada Tells Her Story

was one of her ways of acknowledging her Jewish heritage.

I was jolted back to reality when Mother asked if one's religion should matter. That was something I had never thought about, just accepted. Mother explained that she considered herself Catholic but never gave up acknowledging her Jewish roots. The contradiction for her was that Spain and the Church were denying the Aztecs their religion. Yes, she agreed that human sacrifice should be strictly forbidden, but not because, as the church taught, Christ had been sacrificed for humanity, but because it was inhumane. As for their other gods, she believed it was their right to honor them as had their ancestors. I would have expected an explanation like that from García Bravo. I wondered about myself and how I did not know this side of my mother.

Having had enough of that conversation, I changed the subject and asked Mother about hearing her say I was to be engaged to Jorge Alvarado. I said I couldn't imagine anything better. All my friends were engaged or already married. Of all the Alvarado brothers, I think Jorge was the best. I asked her if Father approved. Mother stopped the barrage of questions, saying the engagement announcement would come out in a month if all went well. The secret menorah had taken on less significance.

Chapter 18

The Big Question

With Cortés back from Honduras, you'd think the colony would have settled down again, but just the opposite. Father would come home every day with reports of discord. He said his appointment as governor was Cortés' way of controlling him. In reality, he claimed; he had no power. Cortés was in charge behind the scenes. He had appointed Gonzalo de Sandoval and Luis de la Torre as co-governors. Sandoval had been in the colony since 1519; he had come to New Spain with Cortés. Torre, said Father, was just a bureaucrat going along with whatever Sandoval wanted. Neither of them, Father grumbled, had come to his aid in the battle against Salazar.

Father held at least one party monthly to appease the colony's wealthy aristocrats. Holding a social event was one of the few ways the rich could spend and display their money, so there were two or three competing events every week.

García Bravo was my escort for most of the city's social functions. Father didn't necessarily approve because he was a civil servant, but he had become a close family friend and was famous for his talent for having the latest gossip. Since we had nothing romantic, Father was satisfied to have someone chaperon me. We looked like father and daughter and often became the center of attention at parties.

What I liked most about him was that he never smelled of sandalwood, a familiar scent used by men and women to cover the scent of body order from clothes infrequently washed. He smelled fresh with no body odor. I knew he had an Aztec bathing area in his Aztec home.

I was fortunate because of Mother's merchant connections. I got first viewing of the fabrics and fashions that came into the clothier. You could say I was a trendsetter for the young aristocratic group. I favored the Isabelle-of-Portugal style that featured an open neckline, a refreshing departure from the stuffy ruff collars popular in Spain. My favorite jewelry was pearls, which I liked to put in my hair. Compared to the current fashions with billowy sleeves and layers of skirts, my style was more understated, with fewer flourishes and ribbons.

My love for chopines, however, was undeniable. These raised cork platform shoes were in high fashion, and I spent hours perfecting my walk and dancing in them so I would not need servants' help. They were the most adorned part of my attire, usually with red ribbons and emboldened with seed pearls. I admit, I was coquettish with my chopines, adjusting my seating position so they would peer out from under my skirt.

My former tutor, Señor Diego, often visited our palace

parties with his cousin, Isabel. She was quite the flirt. I watched him rebuff her attentions but observed them very close on several occasions in private. He misguidedly assumed that because of our parents' professional relationship, he had a chance at courting me. Mother told me that Señora Catalina Albornoz had approached her about an engagement with their son. She had declined because Father was adamant that he was far beneath us.

Diego would make calculated advances when I appeared momentarily alone and tried to swoop me onto the dance floor. Thrown off guard, rather than protest, I would finish the dance. He was an excellent dancer, and we drew attention from onlookers. Finally, with only a hint of politeness, I told Diego he should not ask me to dance again, and if he did, I would make a scene.

On the other hand, Isabel and I grew closer as friends. I never said anything about the situation between her and Diego. I became suspicious that she was pregnant, and Isabel seemed to have vanished shortly after that.

One day, García Bravo asked me if Mother and Father had arranged an engagement for me. I knew he wondered, not for himself, but as a general question. Most young girls of my age and social status were already engaged to be married. The political turmoil of the last two years had left no time for such social endeavors. Discussions with Mother centred on that possibility.

Who might be suitable? Or should I return to Spain for an appropriate marriage prospect?

I told him that arrangements were underway for Jorge Alvarado. He approved, saying that Jorge was a good man, respected by his men, and wealthy. But, in confidence, he shared that Jorge had been married before. This was news to me. How had Father not known this? Indeed, this information should have been available in the *audencia*. When I queried García Bravo, he said the marriage must have been in Spain. Now, of course, was the problem of what happened to this wife. Was she still alive?

Chapter 19

Luisa's & Jorge's Engagement

Mother and Father had done the requisite checks regarding Jorge's character. Father confirmed that Jorge owned the rights to and tributes from a large *encomienda* where he grew wheat! It would be an ideal business partnership with Mother and her grist mill. There was one problem, according to Father: Jorge's previous marriage. I told Mother what García Bravo had told me, and she told Father. He had searched the records of the *audencia* for a record of her death. Nothing. Father would have to talk to Jorge in person and ask him.

There was a change in Father; he now included me in conversations about my engagement. He said it was time I was introduced to the society of Spain because if this engagement failed, I would return to find a suitable husband. I knew little about the Alvarado brothers besides they were First Conquerors. As for Jorge's family in Spain, I knew nothing. I could deduce, however, that with all sons and Jorge being one of the youngest, there would be no inheritance for him. It was fortunate he had made his way in the New World.

Father proposed that the de Estrada name and his position as Treasurer and sometimes governor should carry sufficient weight to approve the engagement from the Alvarado's perspective. Father brought up the topic of my dowry, which would be some ten thousand silver pesos. That was a substantial sum. Mother said that Marina would be coming of age soon and that her engagement and dowry should be just as critical. Father responded with a nod of agreement. I knew Mother was already in the process of making those engagement arrangements for Marina! Lastly, Father stated that "God Willing," the records would indicate the Alvarados were solidly Catholic and not *Conversos*. Hearing that comment, I noticed Mother flinch. I knew that he knew that her extended family were *Conversos*. She chose not to say anything.

The de Estrada mansion was the perfect venue for the engagement party. In Spain, such a party would have been lavish, with hundreds in attendance. Our galas in New Spain were much smaller. Those in our social class numbered fewer than a hundred. The next layer of society, wealthy businessmen or high-rank civil servants like judges, could make up two hundred. Those two layers rarely mixed socially, so our events were more familiar among people we knew.

Cortés rarely attended these parties. On rare occasions, he would show up unannounced. When he did, the women flocked to him; his charm was always alluring. He was undoubtedly the most eligible and prosperous bachelor in the colony if not the whole world.

Never did the native woman and mother of his child accompany him. García Bravo told me she married another Spaniard shortly after going to Honduras with Cortés. Their son, Martin, was taken from her and put in the care of one of Cortés' relatives. I began to doubt that I would ever meet this famed woman.

There were very few women my age and my social status. We were a small group of less than fifteen. Most of us were engaged or already married to wealthy conquistadors. Marriage meant having children and taking care of the household. Each new addition, a prospective bride from Spain, was our delight. We made it our priority to invite them into our enclave and introduce them to this strange new world.

A most recent arrival, a young woman of eighteen named Leonor, was about to transform us from our innocent, prudish ways into more worldly, sophisticated ladies. She was on the edge of our group, but we found her so engaging that we ignored her less-than social standing. You could say she was marrying down to hopefully move up through her intended husband's landholdings and business dealings. She was a shrewd woman.

Leonor reported that the King was incensed with Cortés and threatened to bring him back to Spain in chains. Was it for murder or fomenting civil unrest? Perhaps Jorge would know more about Cortés.

An RSVP to Hernán Cortés: Doña Luisa de Estrada Tells Her Story

When he was in Mexico City, as it was now called, Jorge would be my escort to one of the week's parties as part of our pre-engagement activities. He was never home for long. We seemed to be compatible. My feelings for him only grew; I always thought about him. But Jorge was not nearly as ardent. I tried not to let it bother me, but it did. I wondered if it had anything to do with his previous marriage. On that topic, I waited for Father to converse with Jorge.

He was a handsome man of typical height with clear hazel eyes, light brown hair, and a prominent square jawline. It was his hands that I admired most. Whenever he held my hands in his, they were flawless. He always managed to have them manicured as if he were royalty. As a conquistador who held the reins of his horse and weapons used in battle, I would have thought them rough and scarred. Jorge walked with a slight limp from an injury obtained in one of his conquest battles. Despite his limp, he was an excellent dancer, that is when he rarely danced. He preferred to let me dance with others while he held hospitable conversations with his friends and fellow conquistadors.

I eventually had to ask Mother about the status of Jorge's first marriage. She said she had not heard anything and would ask Father. I later learned from Mother that Father had asked Jorge about it weeks ago. His first wife had died in childbirth in Spain. A relative had adopted the baby. The engagement was on. It would have been considerate of Father to have told me! I was anxious enough as it was.

Marriages of the elite always titillated the aristocracy's hankerings for the rituals of their Spanish homeland. The colony's new rich, primarily conquistadors, considered the invitation an entré into the highest social class.

Another newcomer had arrived in the colony who would thrill the upper crust: Luis de Guzmán y Saavedra. He was the grandson of the Duke of Medina Sidonia and the first royal to come to the colony to take up residence. Our engagement party was used to introduce him to society. To everyone's surprise, it would also announce his engagement to my sister Marina! The Duke was twenty-six, and Marina was eleven. Mother had made all the prerequisite arrangements.

At the ball, the older married adults assembled on one end of the ballroom, while the young unmarried hopefuls gathered closest to the orchestra, eager to dance every dance. Diego Albornoz was among them. Without his cousin, Isabel, he brought a young lady, the daughter of some high-ranking civil servant. Breaking away from her, he seized a moment with me while I was standing alone getting a refreshment. He moved close, put his mouth to my ear, and proclaimed that he was now twenty-two, only two years younger than Jorge. I didn't know what his point was and walked away.

The ball lived up to its promise of being a regal-like event. It was late 1526. Jorge was twenty-four years old, and I was thirteen.

During one of the orchestra breaks, I found Jorge deep in conversation with Father. As I approached, I heard the name 'Cortés. Upon seeing me, they immediately stopped conversing.

Chapter 20
Wedding Invitations

Invitations for the weddings went out by messenger, and a response was required for attendance. We received a 'No' from Cortés without explanation.

There was a tremendous amount of planning to be done. Mother was resting, ready to give birth to her eighth child any day. It had been only four months since the engagement ball. Creating a party to rival the engagement party required talent. The fact that a Duke's son was also engaged to my sister increased the pressure to create an unforgettable event.

To my surprise, I received a letter from Francisco Sanchez. I hadn't recognized the name. Upon opening the letter, I realized it was from Franciso, the boy my age, who was in my tutoring sessions at Cortés' palace. He was writing on behalf of his father, Bartolomé. I couldn't recall ever meeting his father. It was an offer for his theatre troupe to give a private performance for our wedding party. I showed the letter to Mother, asking her if she remembered a Bartolomé. She didn't. I explained that he had a theatre troupe that performed in Mexico City. The performance was called "Into the Oblivion," a farce about the exploits and mishaps of the conquistadors, Aztecs, Franciscans, and Dominicans.

An RSVP to Hernán Cortés: Doña Luisa de Estrada Tells Her Story

Mother wanted to know if they were any good. The fact that they had been invited to come to Spain and perform for the King indicated that they were. I thought it was perfect and answered their letter to set the date.

Jorge was in the city, and we enjoyed a quiet meal together. We sat at a small table near the kitchen at my parent's palace. A fireplace emitted a soft orange glow, highlighting our faces and casting long shadows against the wall. It was cozy. I brought up my regret that Cortés declined the invitation to our wedding. Jorge looked down and took my hands in his. He told me what had transpired between himself and Cortés when they had last met shortly after the engagement announcement. He explained that Cortés asked to meet him at an inn on the city's edge. He said he thought it was about something to do with Pedro, his brother. Instead, he said that Cortés tried to talk him out of marrying me.

I was shocked. Jorge said he didn't know how to answer him. When Jorge asked what his objection was, he said it was because I was the daughter of Alonso de Estrada. When Jorge told Cortés he would marry me, no matter what he thought, Cortés threatened to take one of his *encomiendas* away. Jorge said he knew there was no way for him to follow through because he had no power. To get out of the situation and allow Cortés to save face, he thanked Cortés for his "fatherly" advice and hoped he would change his mind. Just like that, Cortés excused himself.

I asked Jorge if that was what he and Father were discussing at the engagement ball when I happened upon them. Jorge replied that they were talking about something else. When I asked what it was, he said it was about the alleged murder of his wife, Catalina. Jorge was astonished when I said I already knew about it. I asked him if he thought Cortés had done it. He said he'd never seen Cortés out of control like that, but yes, he thought he may have killed her, but he would never say so publicly.

I then asked his opinion about the suspicions that Cortés had something to do with Ponce de Leon's death. That rumor was ludicrous, he replied. The intensity of his answer took me aback. He said that Cortés had nothing to gain from murdering Ponce de Leon. If anything, my father had more to gain; he would likely remain governor. I couldn't imagine my father as a murderer. I forgave Jorge's insinuation as frivolous.

It was late. There were no intimate moments between us that I so longed for.

Chapter 21

Cortés to Spain

Cortés declined an invitation to our wedding. Slights aside, the reality was that he was preparing to leave for Spain. That was his sole focus. He told everyone he had to see the King in person, claiming he was being mistreated. My new friend, Leonor, saw it differently. She and friends in Spain saw Cortés as self-aggrandizing, arrogant, power-hungry, and a threat to the Crown. They expected the King to treat him harshly.

Intending to impress all of Spain, we watched as Cortés amassed a menagerie of the Aztec world: people (dwarfs, jugglers, acrobats), gold, jewelry, feathers, and textiles to take to Spain. The Aztec porters were laden with goods, and the performers, some in costume, trekked to the coast like a caravan.

His departure and the associated fanfare cast a shadow over our wedding festivities, but Jorge and I chose to overlook it. The wedding and party were well attended, but the air was thick with tension.

While Cortés' was away, the colony was on edge. Father felt relief, but he wasn't taking any chances. There were still many Cortés supporters in Mexico.

Father was inundated with constant letters from the Crown, demanding information regarding Cortés' affairs. The pressure was relentless, with Father working twelve-hour days just to keep up. The chaos and disorder were palpable.

Conquistadors built their palaces. Parties followed. Leonor soon married Juan Diaz del Real, a wealthy settler (*poblador*) who was given a small *encomienda* north of the city. He had constructed a lovely home in Mexico City, enabling Leonor to live in the city and socialize with our ladies' group. She became my best friend and confidant.

With Jorge always away, I reverted to my former ways, attending parties with García Bravo. It was never the same as before I married Jorge. I was saddened when García Bravo announced he would leave; his services were needed elsewhere. With Cortés in Spain, he no longer had his advantage. He said he would write, but he never did.

I was busier than ever, working with Mother in our many businesses. We established another gristmill to meet the demands for corn meal; the European settlers had taken a liking to the Aztec corn tortillas. People poured in. The economy needed blacksmiths, carriage builders, candle makers, livestock breeders, and farmers. The Crown did its best to encourage newcomers to settle and grow crops for domestic production and export, especially around Puebla further south.

Leonor opened a millinery, something that she could never have done in Spain; the laws in New Spain were different, allowing women to own a business. She was the perfect businesswoman. She was genuine, intelligent, elegant, and had a great sense of humor. Men favored her hats for their current fashion. Women favored her for her stylish coifs versus hats, per se, that she styled with embedded jewels and feathers, the latest European trend.

I would frequent her shop, ostensibly to accent a new dress but more to ask for marital advice. I was almost fifteen and married for two years, yet Jorge and I rarely had sexual relations. It was concerned. A woman's duty is to marry and have children, but I didn't know how I could get pregnant if Jorge and I did not share a bed because of his frequent trips to the south. It was very distressing. I was concerned there was something wrong with me, that he had another woman, or that he was still in love with his first dead wife. It didn't help that we were living in my parents' palace. Because Jorge was gone most of the time, he proposed that it didn't make sense to build now and that he would consider it when his business in Guatemala with his brother, Pedro, was finished. I found that unsettling. Despite being married for many years, Pedro didn't have any children either. I thought perhaps that was why I hadn't become pregnant; they were infertile. I was to find out that Pedro had a child with a native woman, which started my anxiety about Jorge all over again. It was something I could not discuss with Mother.

Leonor tried to assure me that Jorge's extended absences were the problem, that life and love in New Spain weren't that different from Spain, and that the relationship between men and women has always been fraught with the same issues. She said I was fortunate to be married to a wealthy conquistador who was ultimately a good, respectable man and that, in time, our problems would work themselves out.

Her solution to my problem was to invite our lady's group to her shop once a week for a reading group. The group assured a steady clientele and cemented her social relationship with us. She had ordered a copy of *Celestina* by Fernando de Rojas that we would read together and discuss. None of us had read anything like this tragic tale of love, lust, and trickery. Of course, during our discussions, we would share our trials with our husbands.

Chapter 22

Holy Terror in New Spain

Doña Francisca, Mother's eighth child, was almost a year old in late 1528. Father was now the colony's most experienced government official and lieutenant governor. The past year had been a tumultuous time. The political situation was precarious for my father but also for those who carried the secret of being Jewish. I worried that his deplorable deeds would draw attention to our family, and an enemy of my father, perhaps even Cortés, would accuse Mother of being a crypto-Jew. Everything they built and owned could be in jeopardy; worse, she could be publicly humiliated, even burned at the stake. She confessed to me that her legitimate concern was that the document protecting her was from the previous reign, and she didn't know if it would still hold in King Charles V's court and New Spain if she were accused.

Jorge was back from Guatemala. Finally, we were out of my parents' palace, which had recently been completed. I hoped living in our own home would bring us closer together. We enjoyed a late breakfast in the finely appointed dining room. Sun shone through the east windows, creating a fresh glow. I imagine I glowed, too; we slept together last. Flowers arranged in silver bowls cast colorful reflections on the linen tablecloth. That was one thing I always had at my house-- an abundance of fresh flowers. At the center of the table, I had placed the gold bird given to Father by Ocelotl, the bird that Mother saved from melting, which she then gifted to me because I adored it so much. I placed it atop a square obsidian block. I looked at it with fond memories of my first months in this beautiful land that morning. Jorge was surprised to see it there and asked me where it came from, declaring it must be Aztec and quite valuable.

I told him the story of our encounter in Huitzalipan with Ocelotl. I knew he knew who Ocelotl was. Everyone did. He said that currently, Ocelotl posed a threat to the Church because he practiced witchcraft, and the Inquisition could very well charge him with communing with the devil. I wanted to know what kind of witchcraft. Jorge said many *encomenderos* (owners of *encomiendas*), including himself, used his ability to predict rain to time planting and harvesting. He was so good that they considered him essential for profits.

I told him that Mother and I considered him smart, generous, and fair. We did some textile trading with him shortly after our arrival. Mother sent a shipment of Aztec textiles to her parents' export/import business in Spain that sold immediately. Ocelotl told us that because the Treasury would start taxing him, he would rather quit trading, move out of Mexico City, and live a more Aztec life. We rarely saw him after that. Jorge concluded the Inquisition would get him sooner or later.

An RSVP to Hernán Cortés: Doña Luisa de Estrada Tells Her Story

Our conversation shifted because I expressed the opinion that the Inquisition was concerned with crypto Jews. I brought up the case of Hernando Alonso. He was the largest cattle and pig farmer there in New Spain. He sold us meat for many years. Jorge said he knew him well and that they were compatriots, First Conquistadors. They all knew Hernando was a secret Jew. Many of the First Conquistadors were, said Jorge as he crossed himself. Even his wealth and support from Cortés couldn't protect him. It was a Fray that had accused him of being a Judaizer. He commented that you didn't have a chance if a Fray accused you. My thoughts were that, fortunately, we were friends with Fray Pedro de Gante just in case Mother might need protection.As if he were reading my mind, Jorge asked me if I should be worried about my mother with the Inquisition upon us. I was stunned at the implication. My thoughts raced. If the officials discovered my mother's secret, I wondered how long it would be before it became public. He asked me if I was a secret Jew. I don't know what came over me. Was it anger or rage? I took a hard swing at him, knocking him off his chair. He pulled the tablecloth and settings to the floor as he went down. The servants looked in to investigate the clatter. Jorge shooed them away.

We were both surprised. My rage spent, I slumped to the floor like a cloth doll, heaving with sobs. Jorge drew me close, comforting me and apologizing for what he had said. It was the most intimate moment we had ever had. He stated he had never seen a hint of anything Jewish in the de Estrada palace.

He explained that before we married, his parents investigated my parent's heritage. They learned of my mother's Jewish background and that they were *Conversos*. His parents assumed that since no Jews were allowed in New Spain, and since my parents were effectively sent here by the Crown, the rumors that your mother is a *Converso*, of not too long ago, must not be true. Little does the world know, said Jorge. Hernando Alonso was evidence of that. He said he didn't know of anyone who would want to harm my mother. My fears mainly were allayed.

Jorge scooped me from the floor and carried me to the bedroom. We spent the afternoon making love. Everything seemed right in the world. After a short nap, we had hot cocoa brought to us. It was once the drink of Aztec royalty; the natives Jorge commanded in conquest ventures introduced it to him. Now rested, we began our ritual of catching up on what had transpired in the colony in his absence.

Chapter 23
Nuño de Guzmán

The news about the homeland was never good. The Crown was always out of money, borrowing heavily from Poland and Germany. According to Father, the Crown's fifth of the gold the *audencia* collected and sent to Spain was never enough to please the King or cover his lavish spending. Father would tell us that if there is gold to be found, someone should step up and lead an entrada to find it. The Aztec gold that Cortés had stolen was long gone. Local supplies were dwindling. Father had started a gold mining venture on his *encomienda*, but it produced a minuscule amount of gold.

We hoped for but rarely received news about Cortés. He was still the main topic of gossip, and any tidbit would be enough to start a conversation. We knew he wasn't in chains but was travelling all over Spain, chasing the King. Despite his disagreements with his Highness, they say he was as famous, if not more famous, in Spain. His Aztec menagerie and tales of conquest and life in The New World garnered many invitations from the wealthy. We suspected he was looking for a new wife. There was no one in the colony that he would consider worthy of him.

The two years Cortés spent in Spain passed quickly. In May 1530, Father received a lengthy letter from the Crown. The contents of the letter unsettled us all, especially Father. Cortés was to return, and we should expect him in July. The letter also informed my father that the existing *audencia*, with Father as governor, would be dismantled and replaced with a new entity: The *Real (Royal) Audiencia de México.* To head the new *audencia* would be a President. Effective immediately, the new President would be Nuño de Guzmán, the then-Governor of Paáuco, an area on the Gulf Coast.

Everyone, even I, knew that Cortés and Guzmán were enemies. We wondered why the King chose Guzmán. Was it to punish and humiliate Cortés? There was already unrest in the colony. We wondered what would happen once the two met, especially with Guzmán as President. We would soon find out, as the two were to arrive about the same time. Colonists were elated to have Cortés return but worried about what would happen with his rival in charge of the colony. Another murder was the joke.

Guzmán arrived first. As the outgoing governor, Father was responsible for arranging the welcoming and festivities surrounding the transfer of power. Father asked Mother to please help, and she asked me to help her. We organized most of the arrangements with some assistance from Father's employees at the *audencia*.

Two of Guzmán's two *oidores* (judges) arrived ahead of Guzmán and dictated many of their requirements to honor the incoming President. My interactions with Juan Ortiz de Matienzo and Diego Delgadillo showed that they were not to be trusted. They asked me for special favors and tried to order me around because of my age. Two additional *oidores* might have balanced these two men, but they died right after arriving at port.

Guzmán arrived in the city with banners flying and crowds cheering. The plaza was filled with carriages, their horses outfitted with colorful cloth drapes. The main reception was held at the Catholic Church. Father did not want to host Guzmán at our palace, so I implored Jorge's brother, Pedro, to do it, making the point that it was in his best interest to show he supported Guzmán.

We all attended the social function. Even Jorge was there for the festivities. Father made his presence known at the event with Mother by his side. I was wary Guzmán would use the opportunity to defame Father, but the "President" continued in a jovial but sarcastic manner.

Our social group of aristocrats was cautiously optimistic that order in the colony would be restored, but we were realistically doubtful. Guzmán's reputation as a cruel, greedy man preceded him. He was incredibly exploitative with the natives whom he deemed worthy merely as slaves to sell. Guzmán and slavery, I would learn shortly, involved my father.

Cortés returned with a new title: Marqués del Valle de Oaxaca. Accompanying him was his new young wife, nineteen-year-old, Juana Ramirez y Zúñiga, a high-ranking noblewoman. The marriage surely raised his social status to nobility-- by marriage. We heard the news that they were treated like royalty after disembarking and making their way to Mexico City. In each town they passed through, they were cheered by settlers and Aztecs, shouting "Viva Cortés."

They stayed first at his palace in Coyoacán and then in his palace on the plaza when they arrived in Mexico City. The colonists watched and waited for a chance sighting of the couple.

Chapter 24
Foreboding

The details of what had transpired between the King and Cortés dribbled in. The sentiment was that his new title as Marqués of Oaxaca indicated that the King had clipped his wings. Oaxaca was two days from Mexico City, a distance that would indeed limit his influence. The gossip at social events was all about Cortés and his new wife. Who was she? Was she royalty? Who was she related to? How old was she? Where would they live?

Just days after Guzmán's inauguration, he had Pedro Alvarado arrested. Jorge and I were to find out early the following day. As we woke, there was a frantic knock on our bedroom door. The house servant, a young man from Spain, shouted in desperation that Pedro was asking for Jorge's help.

Jorge quickly dressed. He was about to leave without me, but I insisted he wait for me. I promised I would be quick and could dress without my lady-in-waiting. He was frantic. I thought that if anyone were to be arrested, it would be my father.

The colony was in near anarchy, going from bad under Father's governorship to worse under Guzmán's presidency. I was relieved that Father no longer wielded power. What he had done during his tenure was beyond comprehension. Now, he could no longer bring shame to our family name.

Jorge surmised that Guzmán feared Pedro would gather support for Cortés and against him. The arrest signaled to everyone that they better beware because he was now in charge. Anyone he deemed a threat could be arrested.

When we arrived at the *audencia,* we found Pedro was sequestered at the Franciscan monastery. Our carriage had already left, so we had to hustle there on foot. I was unprepared; my shoes pinched, so I had to remove them and walk barefoot. Jorge did not appreciate the pause.

At the convent, the two *oidores* monitoring Pedro would not allow me in. Jorge was given a brief supervised visit. Afterwards, he pulled me aside so we could not be overheard. He said Pedro was charged with embezzlement and "other" undefined crimes. He said it was good that the *oidores* were listening in because Pedro told him that he and Cortés were no longer friends. Surely, they would report that back to Guzmán, who would consider him less of a threat. He explained that when Pedro was in Spain last year, Cortés expected him to marry his cousin, Cecilia Vázquez. When he didn't and instead married Francisca de la Cueva, who is connected to the Crown, Cortés took it personally.

The story sounded familiar: Cortés had once tried to interfere with our marriage. Jorge took it personally this time when Cortés tried to interfere with his brother's marriage. Maybe Cortés wasn't the man he thought he was, he commented. That was the first time I heard Jorge doubt Cortés' character.

Jorge then gave me the sad news. Since Pedro was locked up, he would have to take on the leadership in Guatemala. I knew our time would be short, but not this short. We were led out, almost kicked out, with the door slamming behind us. Before leaving, he contacted the best legal representation for his brother, and Pedro was eventually released.

The colony was constantly involved in litigious battles: conquistador against conquistador, natives against *encomenderos* (those holding *encomiendas)*, and natives against the *Real Audencia.*

When the *encomenderos* found out that the properties the King had returned to Cortés would be his and his heirs in perpetuity, they were outraged. It was the King's reward to Cortés as the First Conqueror. Cortés had become a wealthy man, and now his heirs would also be rich. We would have to return our estates to the Crown after two generations. The law requiring one to return the *encomienda* to the Crown had always been the understanding, but the wealth obtained from the land and free labor fed an intensified resistance to having to give them back.

Chapter 25

The Year -- 1530

My friends and I eagerly awaited Cortés's invitation to a Grand Ball that would surely happen to celebrate his return and introduce his new wife. The air was thick with excitement. But many weeks passed, and neither Cortés nor his wife were seen leaving his palace. That didn't stop the colony's ladies, who set about getting ready in a conspicuous consumption frenzy of gowns, hats, shoes, and accessories.

Finally, the invitations arrived by messenger, and Cortés' official Marqués seal was predominately displayed.

The Marqués del Valle de Oaxaca -- Hernando Cortés
Requests Your Attendance
for a Reception in Honor of Juana Ramirez y Zúñiga
Join us for a Banquet & Ball
Gifts for All

The local economy hummed with activity. Carriages and the horses were meticulously cleaned and shined. Shoes were expertly cobbled especially for the event, and orders for the latest fabrics from Europe, whose shipment had been delayed, were eagerly inquired about. The Leonor's millinery shop was inundated with

An RSVP to Hernán Cortés: Doña Luisa de Estrada Tells Her Story

requests. The city's seamstresses worked day and night sewing the gowns for the event.

Since Cortés' arrival, Guzmán had maintained a discreet presence; his absence from the festivities would be a foregone conclusion. The tension between the two men was palpable, adding a layer of intrigue to the unfolding events.

Hours before the event, we, as a family, including Jorge, who had been home for a few days, were relaxing in the courtyard. Our calm was interrupted when our servant, who manned the front door, startled us and announced that Guzmán was waiting for Father in the parlor; he had forced his way in. Father grumbled, walking off in a huff. When neither he nor our servant returned, Mother and I went to look for him.

We entered the parlor and found Father transfixed, holding an envelope. When he saw us, he told us that Guzmán insisted he hand deliver it to Cortés at the banquet. When Mother asked what was in the envelope, he raised his shoulders in an "I don't know" manner. He described Guzmán's orders as a threat: Do it or else. He resigned to deliver it that evening.

As the sun set, the plaza suddenly burst into a frenzy of horses and carriages, their hooves echoing on the cobblestones. Our palace was across the plaza, and dressed for the event in our finery necessitated a carriage to avoid the filth left by the many horses. It was a tight fit for the five of us; our dresses took up more than their fair share of space. Father suggested that he and Jorge would walk, leaving Mother, me, and Marina in the comfort of the transport.

Upon arrival, torches lit the façade of the Cortés palace, casting huge shadows against its walls as people approached the front gate. Guards were vigilant on the lookout for Guzmán with orders that he would not be allowed in.

The aristocrats in their glorious gowns poured through the wide-open doors; the chatter was all about the purported gifts from Spain. The orchestra played to calm the crowd and moved quickly between musical selections. Cortés had brought a gifted harpsichordist and an ornate harpsichord back with him. He always meant to impress.

A bell rang, and we ushered into the banquet hall. We were seated around the table, with placards identifying our assigned seats. I watched Father reach Cortés, whisper something, and hand him the envelope. Cortés started to hand it off to one of his servants but then changed his mind, turning from the guests and opening the delivery. Father then made his way to his seat beside us.

The din quieted as we waited for Cortés to give his salutations and at least introduce his new wife. He pivoted and raised his arms to quiet the crowd and welcome his guests. To his right was his beautiful young wife, who was obviously taken with her husband. As she rose, the guest let out an "oooooh," affirming her status and beauty. Self-confidently, she smiled and addressed the attendees. Meanwhile, I observed Cortés scan the room until he located Father. The feast began.

The feast was divine. Cortés had brought back several chefs from Spain. There were platters of broiled turkeys, roast pork, and beef. He had wanted French pastries, but King Charles's war with France made that politically unwise. There was no end to the pouring of the wine. After the meal, the tables were cleared, and the guests looked forward to the ball.

In a dignified way, Cortés stood up, his new wife still sitting beside him. He raised his arms, quieting the guests. He said he wanted to make an announcement. At that point, everyone hushed. He said he had just been informed that Guzmán's government was forcing him to immediately sell his palace so that a National Palace of Mexico could be constructed in its place. The gala that evening would be the last event to be held there. Then he added that he and his wife would be moving to Cuernavaca. He concluded with a toast: "Viva Mexico." The crowd cheered, "Viva Mexico."

The volume of the chatter rose again until another bell rang, and everyone looked his way. In his usually charming bravado, Cortés announced that a card was attached under each person's chair. On the card, they would find their assignment to a specific room in the palace or garden where desserts and fruits would be served. He instructed us to hold onto our cards as they would be needed later. Everyone quickly bent to retrieve their cards and started to rise, delighted with the intrigue. Another bell rang. This time, a servant announced that the guests should proceed to their appointed rooms. Cortés was nowhere to be seen.

We were sorted into rooms of five to fifteen people. I was in a room with the young aristocratic wives, most of my friends, about thirteen of us, hosted by Juana, Cortés' wife. To our delight, there was a fashion show featuring the latest gowns from Spain. Juana selected three beautiful Aztec girls as models. With their hair done up and adorned with jewels, they were stunning. One barely noticed that the women were barefoot.

Juana and I bonded immediately, perhaps because we were close in age and social status. I discovered she was born in Santo Domingo, Hispaniola, so she was familiar with living in a world similar to New Spain. Juana conveyed that she found the whole of New Spain beautiful and the people kind. She marveled at the plaza and the swiftness with which the city had replaced the Aztec temples. Those she wished she could have seen. From my perspective, Juana was more like me than any other Spanish woman in the colony. She outranked me but treated me as her equal.

Mother later told me she was in a room with the older

aristocratic wives. They tended to gossip, which she detested. The subject of that evening's conversation was about the gifts that were to come later. The ladies were given the second showing of the beautiful gowns Juana brought from Spain.

Father said his card assigned him to a parlor with five other dignitaries. Cortés, himself, was the host. He announced that he was serving sherry gifted to him by the King. Grapes and cheese were the complement. According to Father, Cortés seemed in fine spirits and made a special effort to address him. As for the envelope, Cortés said nothing.

After a while, a gong rang, and everyone was encouraged to gather in the ballroom so the festivities could begin. We were reminded to keep our cards safe. The evening proceeded with frivolity and without incident.

Again, the gong sounded just before midnight, and the evening was drawn to a close. Cortés and Juana thanked everyone for their attendance, and they exchanged well-wishes. Cortés announced that he and Juana would be at the front gate and dispense gifts for everyone in exchange for their card. That caused a stir and encouraged the people to hasten to leave rather than dawdle and chit-chat.

Cortés stood on one side of the palace gate, Juana on the other. Each was holding a blue velvet bag secured by a woven gold cord. As the attendees passed towards the entrance, they handed a servant their card, then passed to Cortés and Juana, who personally gave them a freshly minted gold escudo coin. It was worth sixteen *reales*, an astonishing sum to be given away as a gift.

Chapter 26

What Hath Transpired?

As we waited for our carriage, the cool, crisp air of night felt good after the night of dancing and frivolity. Father was most indignant, criticizing Cortés for giving away such a valuable coin. He claimed Cortés must be up to something. He turned to us and demanded we give him our coins. Of course, Mother handed hers over, as did Marina. When he turned to me, I flatly refused. He didn't try and get Jorge's coin.

Fortunately, our transport arrived, and we seated ourselves; this time, we were not worried about rumpling our gowns. Father tapped the roof to let the driver know we were ready. I made a comment that afterward, I wished I hadn't. I claimed that as the Marqués, who lived days from the city, Cortés would have little influence from that far away. He now had a wife, too. Then, I made a critical error in mentioning that Juana had invited me to their palace next week. I was about to continue, but that was enough to get Father going. He said under no circumstances was I to socialize with Cortés' wife. Sitting next to me in the cramped carriage, Jorge squeezed my hand, which was covered by my gown. I know it was meant as a restraint to continue the conversation, but it was the most intimate gesture of affection I had had from him since he arrived. I was satisfied to stay silent and enjoy the closeness of my husband.

We retired to our respective bedrooms when we arrived home, but the night was short-lived. Just two hours after all the candles were extinguished, Mother shrieked, calling for help.

We made a mad rush to her chamber, stopping in the doorway to see Father sprawled on the floor at the foot of the bed. Jorge bent to check him for signs of life and proclaimed he was dead. I asked what happened. Mother said that after arriving home, Father came banging against the door frame and stumbling into her room. He was gasping for breath and clutching his chest. She said she heard him hit the floor with a thud. That's when she yelled for us and lit a candle.

By then, a couple of servants had arrived. They covered his body with a bed covering and dragged him out of the room on the rug where he had landed. There was nothing more to be done until morning. Jorge retired, and I climbed onto the bed with Mother to learn more about what had transpired.

She explained that Father said he wasn't feeling well and probably ate too much at that banquet. He hoped to feel better in the morning. It was a good time to tell Mother my theory about Cortés. I asked her if she thought Cortés had something to do with Father's death. I said it was a coincidence that Father gave him that sealed envelope and then was in Corte's small group at the gala. Then he

An RSVP to Hernán Cortés: Doña Luisa de Estrada Tells Her Story

was dead.

Mother was taken aback, saying that my idea was far-fetched. I said I knew that she knew Father had always been afraid of Cortés. Since Guzmán arrived, Father has been anxious. I didn't know who he was more afraid of -- Guzmán or Cortés? In any event, I asked her if she noticed at the banquet that after Father gave Cortés that sealed envelope, Cortés scanned the room until he found where Father was sitting. If looks could kill, they did, I said, because Father was dead!

Mother replied she'd noticed Cortés was occupied with something but hadn't seen him eying Father. As for that envelope, she said we'd never know what was in it, but it probably had to do with Guzmán's plan to build a national palace. She wanted to go to sleep, promising to continue our discussion the next day.

I was unwilling to let go of the conversation and brought up the death, the murder, of Cortés's first wife. I vowed then that someday, I would make sure that Cortés is charged with her murder because it's true.

Mother assured me there would be an investigation as to the cause of Father's death. She ended our conversation by warning me not to get involved with the mess surrounding the death of his first wife because, after all, he was found innocent. I concluded that his wife, Juana, needs to know who she married.

News of Father's death shocked the community. Rumors spread, and people suggested that Cortés had something to do with it. An inquiry was initiated. Likewise, the government began an audit of Father's Treasury accounts, as was protocol.

Jorge was back from Guatemala. We were leading a calmer marital life. With no children, we enjoyed playing with my sister, Francisca. As we watched little Francisca attempting to walk on the parlor's thick carpet, I brought up the possibility that Cortés had murdered my father. I said I didn't believe the official claim that Father had died of natural causes.

Jorge said I needed to evaluate my assertion rationally. He explained that my father had been under tremendous stress for more than ten years. He was appointed governor, replaced, arrested, and appointed again. Then Guzmán arrived! That much stress would surely take a toll on a person. He concluded that maybe he ate too much at the gala and died of natural causes.

I asked him what he thought about the deaths of Ponce de Leon and then Marcos de Aguilar. Jorge doubted that Cortés had anything to gain from their deaths. He may have been infuriated with the rejection by the King for appointing them but killing or poisoning either of them would not have benefited him. He pointed out that Aguilar, particularly right before his death, named your father governor as his successor.

That was exactly my point. Cortés wanted my father out of the way so he could be governor. Another possibility is that Cortés was so angry and humiliated that he sought revenge, waiting for the right moment. Jorge said not being appointed might have been enough to enrage him, but not to the level of murder. It's known that he has a violent temper, but those supposed murders would have taken calm patience, planning, and execution. No one observed any untoward behavior between Cortés and any of these men, including your father. Again, I said that was my point.

Then Jorge turned the conversation, suggesting that my father stood the most to gain from Aguilar's death. When Jorge saw the horrified look on my face, he added that even though my father had been somewhat erratic those last few years, he couldn't imagine my father murdering anyone.

Chapter 27

Not in This Church

Father's death created a plethora of problems for Mother. Her immediate concern was to get my father buried. He had paid the church for an above-ground family niche. When she contacted them about the burial, they refused to allow it. No persuasion could change their mind: Alonso de Estrada was not welcome. Time was of the essence. He had been dead for two days.

My thoughts were that God was punishing my father for his evil deeds. I could see why the church didn't want him buried there. Mother disagreed, saying father was a devout Catholic. He was a good man and did as he needed to do. I disagreed. Devoutness did not make up for avarice and greed.

Jorge suggested they could bury my father at Tepapayeca, his *encomienda*. It was about seventy-one miles southeast of the city, far enough away to deter looters and least likely to be observed.

Months passed, and still, the church would not change its stance. Finally, Mother pleaded for help from Queen Juana to force the agreement with the church. Only then, with a royal order from the Crown, was the audencia required to make the church honor their original arrangement. Servants were sent to dig up the grave and return his body to Mexico City. My father was finally laid to rest. It was almost a year since his death.

One of the more critical problems for my mother was that she no longer had access to my father's yearly royal salary of almost 1,500 silver pesos. It was not a paltry sum. It was high enough that the Crown deemed it sufficient to preclude temptation to engage in corrupt practices. Ha! My father was owed almost four months' salary, nearly 4,000 silver pesos, at his death. But the *audencia* would not release it.

As per the rules of the legal investigation, Mother was informed that if Father's treasury ledgers had any irregularities or monies unaccounted for, she, as his wife, was responsible for covering them. Her problem was that the *audencia* would not allow her to cover them personally. Instead, Guzmán ordered all her goods and properties to be seized and sold to pay the balance due. At the time, goods were sold for twenty percent of their value. Mother pled with them to let her pay. When they refused, her legal representatives managed to enact a stay while she attempted to reconcile the accounts.

During the investigation, it appeared that my father had sent 45,000 silver pesos from the Treasury to Spain in 1524, right after our arrival. That was three years' worth of salary! A notation in the ledger indicated the amount was for the care of his three children they had left behind in Spain: Luis Alfonso, Juan Alfonso, and Ana.

Mother was floored. For that, the *audencia* ordered her property in Ciudad Real in Spain to be confiscated as collateral.

It was only with the help of her connections to the Crown that she was finally able to get some relief. She petitioned Queen Juana, once again, to intervene. The result was that 550 silver pesos were forgiven outright. The Queen ruled that my mother could personally pay whatever was owed with the caveat that if there were a judgment against her, she would have to pay it in gold. As for the outstanding 45,000 pesos, the audencia insisted the debt be paid, but in the end, the Queen forced them to cancel the enormous debt. Unfortunately for my mother, my father's past owed salary was never released. Mother's properties in Cuidad Real, Spain, including her dowry, could not be attached and were returned.

Jorge and I were astounded by my mother's connection with Queen Juana. He asked me if I had always known about this relationship. I knew my mother and Queen Juana had a personal correspondence, but I never thought to question their relationship. Now, I realized how significant it was. I said my mother always claimed that keeping your allies as friends is essential as you may need them someday. If it hadn't been for the Queen, Mother would likely have lost her home. That conversation further dampened my fears that Mother could ever be charged as a Converso. She would have the protection of the Crown.

Chapter 28

A Way of Life

When I entered my home after visiting with my friends at Leonor's millinery, there was an unexpected delight on the entry table—a pineapple! The house servant informed me it was a gift from a native man named Martín Ocelotl. My heart skipped a beat. *"Una pina,"* I exclaimed. I bent over to inhale its sweet fragrance. It was a treasure, a delicacy sought after in Europe, but the long journey across the ocean made such requests impossible to fulfil. By the time the pineapple arrived, it was spoiled.

Accompanying the pineapple was a letter. I was surprised. Could it be true? Could Martin now read and write in Spanish? I took the unopened letter and went upstairs to my private quarters. With a mix of curiosity and anticipation, I unfolded the letter. Perhaps he had someone write this for him, I mused. It looked so Spanish.

July 1531

Dear Doña Luisa:

You have been a valued friend for many years. Our worlds have changed since I first met you and your family in Huitzilapan. Among the

Spaniards, I believe you know and respect my people's way of life.

In Texcoco, we have been able to live our lives as Nahuas, but that is changing. The Franciscans are becoming more demanding. I believe these friars to be *tzitzimeh*, who are bewitching my people. As of late, the friars are saying the *tzitzimeh* are the devil of their Christian faith. It is another of their clever ways to trick us.

These Christians are forcing us to give up our wives and choose only one. We are watched to see if we engage in our Nahua rituals. Now, because there are so many of them, they are exposing us as idolaters. The consequences can be severe. They are taking away our properties, our homes.

We are resisting as best we can, but we need to fight these Spaniards with Spaniards. As a friend and someone who appreciates our way of life, I pray you can assist me and help us find a Spanish lawyer who can defend us and understand us as a people.

Sincerely, Martin Ocelotl

It had been years since we worked with or visited our Aztec friend. He had left his way of life behind as a trader, choosing to reside in Texcoco, further from the Treasury's prying eyes. The traditional ways of the natives were now facing the stern gaze of the Church. It wasn't just the Franciscans but the Dominicans and Augustinians who had come to proselytize. They built churches in ever smaller towns. Ocelotl and his people could not avoid them

An RSVP to Hernán Cortés: Doña Luisa de Estrada Tells Her Story anymore.

I knew trying to defend the indigenous peoples was an impossibility; the Church and the Crown held an absolute belief that the Aztecs were pagans. The Franciscans were so concerned with the coming of the end, which was not something I believed, that their mission was to save them all before they died. It would be futile to try and find a lawyer to help Ocelotl's people defend their religion. But if the friars were stealing their properties, that I believed could be defended.

With that thought, I went downstairs to find the gold bird from Ocelotl. I hadn't seen it in some time. At last, it emerged from its hiding place, and I positioned it upon its obsidian pedestal. I sat at the table and admired the bird until I realized I was looking at myself. The obsidian was like a mirror. Indeed, I had heard the natives use this polished stone as a mirror.

I asked myself: What do I believe? It was an existential moment. Did I respect the religion of the Aztecs? Or was I a hypocrite? As long as the natives were at a distance or engaged as servants, I could live my privileged life. My friend, Ocelotl, and his people were facing the destruction of their way of life. Now, I could see the parallels between his situation and the situation of Jews, like my mother's family, who were forced to leave Spain or convert to Christianity. She may appear a devout Catholic, but her deep roots are Jewish! Perhaps that is what will happen with the Aztecs.

I reflected on what my family did to *Xitlali*, separating her from her son in Huitzilapan. I decided to ask if Fray de Gante could offer *Tonatiuh* a position at his craft's school –if the boy wanted to. I would be willing to donate substantially to the school for this favor. We hadn't left Mexico City and visited *Huitzalipan* since we arrived. He must be a young man, perhaps even married, by now. I would have to consider that possibility as well. I doubted that Cortés' staff would let *Xitlali* return. She had become indispensable, especially since she had learned to speak Spanish.

I invited Mother to view my latest acquisitions for the oratory in our palace. It was austere but serene and comfortable. I wanted it large enough to accommodate fifteen. I commissioned an altar and crucifix from Fray de Gante, giving Aztec craftsmen a project to work on. Mother thought the room was beautiful. It was perfect for me but not for her, she said.

She asked if we could go to the parlor for privacy; she had news to share. She reminded me of the Crown's broken promise to my father. When he was appointed Treasurer, the Crown agreed that my brother, Luis Alonso, would succeed him. Then, the Crown reneged on the agreement. Mother said trying to fight it would be futile. The loss of that royal connection was a blow to our family's social status.

She said she had found a solution to that unfortunate situation. Actually, she had found two solutions: one for herself and the other for my sister Ana, who was in Spain. I was intrigued.

She said she had arranged for Ana's engagement to Juan Alonso de Sousa y Cabrera, the newly appointed Treasurer! I remembered meeting him at Guzmán's induction ceremony. He seemed much older than she. Mother said he was thirty-three, twenty years older than Ana, but that should not be a problem. Her upbringing at the monastery in Spain had prepared her well for her role as an aristocratic wife. She was set to arrive in a month. The wedding was planned for later in the year.

My mother was satisfied because the marriage would keep her connections to the government. Juan Alonso's father was the governor of the Canary Islands, which would elevate her status. After all these years, I was delighted to meet my sister and offered to host their engagement party.

After some chit-chat, Mother asked after Juana Cortés. Had we gotten together? Unfortunately, I explained, it never happened. Juana had sent a letter stating that she had given birth to twins, who had died shortly after birth. She and Cortés had been in Cuernavaca constructing their new palace for some time now. I lamented that I had hoped to ask her if she knew what was in that envelope Guzmán made Father deliver to Cortés. I was sure it contained something important.

Chapter 29

Things Come to a Head

Even though my sister Ana married Juan de Sousa, Mother still faced Guzmán's persistent claims that she owed money to the treasury. Her representatives did what they could.

Guzmán and his *oidores* were unethical at every turn. The colonists watched in horror as some who dared to challenge the them were arrested and tortured. One was hanged and quartered. Another had his foot cut off and whipped. One of Guzmán's most steadfast challengers was the Franciscan priest Juan de Zumárraga. When he arrived, Fray de Gante introduced him to Mother and me. We found them to be kindred spirits. He was a well-educated, well-connected, wise man who came to New Spain in support of the natives. Immediately, a power battle ensued between Guzmán, the natives, and the new priest.

Mother, now the head of the household, gathered us and our spouses at the de Estrada palace to discuss the political situation and ways to protect our businesses. Juan had gone into a mining business with my husband. We would meet regularly to discuss the situation in the colony, with the doors guarded and no servants permitted in that section of the palace.

Our immediate concern was circumventing Guzmán's ban

on letters bound for New Spain. Only approved correspondence could leave the country. We colonists realized that our complaints to the Crown were never heard because they had been seized. To have one's letter intercepted was dangerous because Guzmán would know who his enemies were if the writer had dared to sign the document.

At one of our meetings, the topic of conversation was how Guzmán became President. The men said he was not qualified; he had no training as a lawyer nor experience in the Indies. Jorge proposed that because he had been a member of Charles V's guard, perhaps the King owed him a favor. The others considered the point but concluded that that was hardly enough to warrant his promotion to the highest rank in New Spain.

We women of the family followed in Mother's footsteps. We were well-versed in business, but politics was left to the men. While the men offered their opinions on political matters, the women gathered separately to discuss family or business matters.

I was sitting with my sisters and got up to get some refreshments. I overheard the men discussing the plight regarding Guzmán's ban on communication. It was then that I realized the seaman, Gilberto, could be a solution. I knew we could trust him to get a letter to the King. He could be our savior. I decided to inject myself into the men's group.

I ventured over and stood behind Jorge. The men continued without acknowledging me until I politely interjected that I knew of a way to get a message to the King. That stopped the conversation. I explained my connection to Gilberto. Some of the group members nodded positively, while others were skeptical. It was very risky. They wanted to know more about Gilberto. I told them he was a seaman on my voyage to New Spain, that we had stayed in contact, and that he could be trusted. He makes two sailings a year to and from the colony. Jorge assured the rest that he had met Gilberto at our wedding.

It was the right time of year for him to be in New Spain. Although it was risky, it was our only means of secure communication. The men began to formulate a plan. By this time, the women came to look for me and were appraised of what had transpired. We were now a consolidated group. They decided who should write the letter and its contents. Juan de Sousa was excluded because he was too close to Guzmán. We were afraid that the tiniest implication that he was involved in our secret activities would find him arrested at best and dead at worst. Jorge and I were charged with locating Gilberto.

That evening, we celebrated. We had been under extreme duress for a year. We retreated to the aviary, where the smell of the earth and foliage created a sense of terra firma. We were optimistic.

Chapter 30
The Slave Trade

Mother needed to employ legal investigators to determine the extent of Father's financial dealings in Pánuco, shortly after we arrived in New Spain. The investigators scoured the records in Mexico City and Pánuco to document my father's engagement in the slave trade, something Mother was unaware of.

In 1524, Pánuco was Nuno Guzmán's territory. King Charles had appointed him governor there. Cortés heavily contested that appointment and his authority.

The value of this land, for Guzmán, Cortés, and my father, was slaves who were sold to the West Indies in places like Jamaica, where the indigenous population was depleted due to deaths from harsh conditions, overwork, or disease. To trade in slaves, one needed a license. These could only be granted by the governor. With a license, the holder could capture, brand, and sell slaves. Licenses were often granted to friends so that kickbacks could be hidden. Profits were high. Since the Crown disapproved of the slave trade, much of this activity was poorly documented.

According to the investigators, in 1524, the Royal Governor of Jamaica, Franciso de Garay, needed more slaves for gold mining and pig raising. He objected to the prices Guzmán was charging for slaves and devised a plan to capture and export his own. He organized a 600-man expedition to establish a colony on the Pánuco River. He came into a legal conflict with Cortés, who asserted he claimed that land. Garay traveled to Mexico City to negotiate with Cortés. According to the investigation, Cortés greeted and invited him to dine at his palace. It was Christmas. Two days later, he was dead! Rumors floated that he had been poisoned.

I was about to give up on my conviction that Cortés had something to do with Father's death and all the other rumored deaths that coincided with dining with the famous conquistador. That was until I heard the story of Franciso de Garay. Mother reported the findings in Pánuco about Francisco Garay at the regular family gathering. The husbands and wives sat together for a meal and exchanged the latest news about Guzmán and the colony. For me, that revelation was like a bolt of lightning. It was yet another death of someone who crossed hairs with Cortés!

My thoughts were that anyone who stands in his way, who incites his anger, will find themselves dead. Yes, he was cold and calculating, putting on an amiable front while anticipating and calculating an effective poison to do away with his real or perceived enemy. Did he do it himself, or did he have a servant do it? I wondered. I decided he did it himself!

As in the other cases of suspicious deaths, little, if anything, came of the death of Franciso de Garay. The death of his first wife, Catalina, was investigated, but in the end, he was not convicted. In that case, Cortés was out of control and acted angrily. The other deaths, however, I concluded, were acts of vengeance, cold and calculating. Jorge's argument that Cortés had nothing to gain from Ponce de Leon or Aguilar's deaths no longer held sway. It was then that I decided that one way or another, I would bring Cortés to justice. I thought it best to keep the topic to myself.

Chapter 31
Resolution

Jorge and I had little trouble finding Gilberto, the seaman. As a favor to me, he was more than willing to sneak a message to the Crown by getting it through Guzmán's blockade. We would find out months later when he returned to New Spain he had taken our letter, rolled it up, sealed it in wax, and put it into the contents of a keg that was explicitly addressed to the King only. We didn't know if it was our letter or someone else's that escaped Guzmán's oversight, but the King's reaction was fast and hard. The Crown threatened to replace the entire administration of the *Real Audencia.*

Juan de Sousa was present in the *audencia* when the news from the King arrived. When the family gathered at the de Estrada palace, Juan shared the King's admonishment. We were pleased but wary because Guzmán was still in power, and he could seek revenge on those he deemed traitors. We remained on guard, our optimism tempered by the harsh reality of the situation.

Guzmán, in a surprising turn of events, responded to the King's threat in a manner no one could have predicted. According to Juan, he brazenly took (stole) 10,000 pesos from the treasury and launched an entrada, forcibly conscripting four hundred men to accompany him. His audacious goal was to conquer the area north and west of Mexico City, a move that left everyone in shock and anticipation of what would come next.

Our husbands said, "Good riddance." Guzmán's *oidores* retreated without their heavy-weight president to back them up. There was a brief calm.

Juan shared news from the *audencia* that Guzmán had been successful in his conquest, naming the conquered area New Galicia. When he returned to Mexico City, he sent a letter to the Crown. In his letter, according to Juan, was a request (an expectation) that he be named "Governor of Greater Spain!"

We believed the King would not betray his people in New Spain by expanding Guzmán's reign or naming him Governor. Over our evening meal, Juan was asked question after question about Guzmán. The critical question was: Did he find gold?

Juan said no gold was reported, but Guzmán went on a rampage of enslaving the natives. We concluded that there was no justification for the Crown to give Guzmán the title he wanted, but we would not let our guard down until Guzmán was out of power.

We found out later that Queen Juana had received Guzmán's letter (King Charles was temporarily out of Spain). Her response was to name him the Governor of New Galicia. That was the beginning of the end for Guzmán.

An RSVP to Hernán Cortés: Doña Luisa de Estrada Tells Her Story

By January 1531, a seasoned administrator, Sebastian Ramirez de Fuenleal, was appointed the new President of *the Real Audencia of Mexico*. Nominated by the bishop of Badajoz, Jorge's hometown, Fuenleal was known for his legal expertise, honesty, and honor. Four *oidores*, who were also legally trained and experienced, were named to support him. Handpicked by the Crown, this new administration instilled hope that justice would finally prevail in the colony. Most significant to the Crown was Fuenleal's stance on protecting the rights of Indians and punishing those who mistreated them.

As President, his first order of business was to begin investigations of the members of the *First Real Audiencia*, namely Guzmán and his two *oidores*. We concluded that under Fuenleal, Guzmán would get his just desserts for his grave maltreatment and enslavement of indigenous people. We also learned that Cortés, now a Marqués, was to be investigated.

To Mother's advantage, Queen Juana continued to intercede on her behalf. Mother maneuvered through the new courts under Fuenleal and secured her properties and *encomienda* by claiming her widowhood. Her status as a widow entitled her to the guardianship of her children and their properties as heirs of Alonso's estate. Our de Estrada family was whole again.

Chapter 32

The Envelope

By 1535, the colony under President Fuenleal burst forth with new vigor. The number of social events quadrupled, commerce increased, and new arrivals began an economic boom. Guzmán was not forgotten, but we colonists wanted to move on.

Guzmán, an intriguing figure, was occasionally spotted at the *audencia* during his *residencia* (investigation). Juan de Sousa regularly reported the latest details from the proceedings against Guzmán to the family. One of his tidbits of information was able to finally shed light on my enduring suspicion of what was in that envelope Guzmán made my father give to Cortés at his gala.

According to Juan, when Cortés returned from his two-year stint in Spain, now a Marqués, he and Guzmán engaged in a wily game of cat and mouse. One of Guzmán's initial decrees was to bar Cortés from the city. If he tried, he would be arrested. The problem for Guzmán was that the decree needed to be hand-delivered. He had tried to get his oidores to do his bidding, but they were rebuffed. He couldn't do it since his opportunity to see Cortés in person would have been his gala, but Cortés purposely did not invite him. He must have known that Cortés would have his guards ready in case Guzmán tried to enter or use his position to force his way in. His only opportunity was to get my father to deliver the decree for him.

At that point, I realized, at last, the significance of what was in the envelope. I felt my heart flutter, and I unconsciously jumped up from my seat at the table. Everyone looked my way; Juan paused his telling of the events. Not knowing what to do next, I sat back down, and Juan began again. I felt like I was deaf. I couldn't hear anything. I could see his mouth moving. Then everything went blank. I fainted.

The family rushed to my aid as I crumpled on the floor. When I finally gained consciousness, my head was in Jorge's lap. He was holding my hand and calling my name. When he asked me what had happened, I realized he had not made the connection to what Juan had revealed about the envelope and my determined need to know what was in it all these years. I looked over to Mother. She nodded. She knew my quest had been solved.

The evening resumed, but Jorge and I excused ourselves and returned home. As we walked home, I processed what I had just learned. The walk was like the ticking of a metronome, where I put each element of what had transpired in place. I concluded that when Cortés received the envelope from my father, he must have assumed he was aligned with Guzmán. That look I observed Cortés giving my father was a prelude to his death. The investigation into my father's death did not indicate foul play, but I concluded that it was just luck on the part of Cortés that his nemesis, my father, died.

My rumination ended abruptly when Jorge asked me if I was okay. Now totally aware of my thoughts and implied accusations and aware that the subject was closed as far as the investigation into my father's death was concerned, I replied that I was just fine, that it had been a long day, and I was looking forward to being alone with him.

Chapter 33

Serendipity

I had taken a carriage with my sister Ana to visit the milliner and clothier. She had become my favorite sister and confidant. I took it upon myself to educate Ana about the Aztec culture. I wanted to instill respect for the natives to counter the negative perspective of many. We were in no hurry. Jorge and her husband Juan would likely arrive home late, if at all. Their mining ventures would likely keep them away.

I was at the clothier, eying the latest row of imports. Looking through the fabrics, I asked the merchant to inspect a bolt of green silk damask. As he reached to retrieve the bolt, two customers nearby mentioned Cortés' name. It's not that the name Cortés was rarely mentioned anymore because he was still a frequent source of conversation. It was the hushed tones of the conversers that drew my attention.

I turned slightly to see who they were. They looked to be a mother and a daughter, well-dressed, indeed of higher social status, but not in our social circle. Turning back, I listened more intently while fingering the fine cloth. The older one, the mother, told the daughter that if only she had the money to hire well-appointed attorneys, she would file a civil suit against Cortés. That caught my interest. The woman's last comment sent a bolt of lightning through me. The woman said, "If the criminal courts were not going to find him guilty of Catalina's death, she would find a way. He murdered your sister!"

At that moment, I realized that the older one must be Catalina's mother, and the younger one must be Catalina's sister.

I wanted to approach them but stopped myself. Getting mixed up with people I did not know was not a good idea. I had to consider my next move carefully. I asked the clerk for another bolt to give me something to do and waited. The two women bought some trim and left the shop.

Since my family owned the shop, I was on good terms with the shopkeeper. I inquired if he knew who the two women were. Indeed, he did. They were long-time customers. Suarez was their name. That confirmed my suspicions. The women were who I thought they were.

I thanked the owner and persuaded Ana to return home. Even though she and I had become close, I chose not to share my discovery. On the way home, we chatted. It took everything not to explode and spill my story.

The topic of Cortés and the murders did not go well with Jorge. In the interest of our relationship, I decided to work through a third party to verify that they were who I suspected them to be and then to confidentially fund the fees for the Suarez attorneys and court case. My name was never to be mentioned.

But just as important, I did not want to spoil Jorge's current state of joy. I was finally pregnant with our first child.

Kimberly A. Folse

About the Author

Kimberly A. Folse is a retired academic sociologist and as a second career, she enjoys teaching English as a Second Language (ESL). As the majority of her students are from Mexico, she has come to develop a deep respect for their history and culture.

In particular, Dr. Folse has a keen interest in researching the Conquest of the Aztecs by Hernán Cortés and the significance of colonization for the aristocratic Spaniards who came to develop and rule the colony.

Select Sources & Further Reading

Aguilar-Morena, Manuel. 2007. *Handbook to Life in the Aztec World*. Oxford University Press. New York, New York.

Altman, Ida. 1991. Spanish Society in Mexico City After the Conquest. *Hispanic American Historical Review*. 71(3) 413-445.

Del Castillo, Bernal Diaz. 2012. *The True History of the Conquest of New Spain*. Hackett Publishing, Indianapolis, Indiana.

Lanyon, Anna. 2003. *The New World of Martin Cortes*. Da Capo Press, Cambridge, MA.

Flint, Shirley Cushing. 2013. *No Mere Shadows: Faces of Widowhood in Early Colonial Mexico*. University of New Mexico Press. Albuquerque, New Mexico.

Riley, Michael G. 1965. *The Estate of Fernando Cortes in the Cuernavaca Area of Mexico, 1522-1547*. A dissertation. University of New Mexico. Albuquerque, New Mexico.

León-Portílla. 2002. *Bernardino.De Sahagun: First Anthropologist*. University of Oklahoma Press, Norman, Oklahoma.

Pagden, Anthony. 1986. *Hernan Cortes: Letters from Mexico*. Yale University Press (Revised Edition). New Haven,

Connecticut.

Thomas, Hugh. 2003. *Rivers of Gold: The Rise of the Spanish Empire, from Columbus to Magellan*. Random House, New York, New York.

Townsend, Camilla. *Fifth Sun: A New History of the Aztecs*. Oxford University Press. New York, New York.

Thomas, Hugh1993. *Conquest: Montezuma, Cortes, and the Fall of Old Mexico*. Touchstone. New York, New York.

Thomas, Hugh. 2010. *The Golden Empire: Spain, Charles V, and the Creation of America.* Random House. New York, New York.

Valencia, Robert Y Valencia. 1991. *The Encomenderos of New Spain 1521-1555*. University of Texas Press, Austin, Texas.